A Jake McGreevy Novel

Celtic
Run

SEAN VOGEL

best wishes *S Vogel*

MB PUBLISHING

ISBN, softcover: 978-0-9624166-9-9

ISBNs, E-books:

epub: 978-0-9624166-7-5

fixed layout epub with audio: 978-0-9850814-0-9

mobi: 978-0-9624166-8-2

Library of Congress Control Number: 2012936347

Photo Credits

Cover: Ruby © istockphoto.com/Rozaliya; Paper © istockphoto.com/desuza.
communications; Map © istockphoto.com/bubaone; Background © istockphoto.
com/hudiemm; Title Page: Cliffs © istockphoto.com/ingmar wesemann; Chapter 1:
Passport © istockphoto.com/Booka1; Chapter 2: Starfish:© istockphoto.com/Olivier
Blondeau; Chapter 3: Table Setting © istockphoto.com/studiocasper; Chapter
4: Apple © istockphoto.com/ZoneCreative; Chapter 5: Bike © istockphoto.com/
hiro-pm; Chapter 6: Keyboard © istockphoto.com/David Gunn; Chapter 7: Tickets
© istockphoto.com/david franklin; Chapter 8: Ice Cream Cones © istockphoto.
com/Hakan Dere; Chapter 9: Life Preserver © istockphoto.com/Sam Woolford;
Chapter 10: Key © istockphoto.com/samxmeg; Chapter 11: Limes © istockphoto.
com/ansonsaw; Chapter 12: Rugby Ball © istockphoto.com/Oliver Hamalainen;
Chapter 13: Notebook and Pencil © istockphoto.com/Talaj; Chapter 14: Gum
© istockphoto.com/Jiri Hera; Chapter 15: Glasses © istockphoto.com/clubfoto;
Chapter 16: Water Splash© istockphoto.com/kedsanee; Chapter 17: Yellow Flowers
© istockphoto.com/Cristian Baitg; hapter 18: Biscuits © istockphoto.com/Mostafa
Hefni; Chapter 19: Bench © istockphoto.com/Oksana Samuliak; Chapter 20:
Suitcase © istockphoto.com/John Solie; Chapter 21: Cell Phone © istockphoto.
com/Brandon Laufenberg; Chapter 22: Chocolate Syrup © istockphoto.com/
ALEAIMAGE; Chapter 23: Window © istockphoto.com/Geoffrey Holman; Chapter
24: Ruby © istockphoto.com/Rozaliya; Chapter 25: Flashlight © istockphoto.com/
Petr Malyshev; Chapter 26: Rope © istockphoto.com/gokhan ilgaz; Chapter 27:
Wagon Wheel © istockphoto.com/Artsem Martysiuk; Chapter 28: Horse Shoes ©
istockphoto.com/Deborah Cheramie; Chapter 29: Payphone © istockphoto.com/
Daniel Stein; Chapter 30:Bandaid © istockphoto.com/Igor Skrynnikov; Epilogue:
Plane © istockphoto.com/Okea; End Page: Rainbow © picturescolourlibrary.com/
Stock Connection

For Sara,
You are my inspiration, my breath, my home

Chapter 1

Jake clenched his fists. Zach was sauntering down the airplane aisle as if he were the best thing since the iPod. *Everyone has an archenemy,* Jake thought. *Luke Skywalker has Darth Vader. Harry Potter has Voldemort. Me? I have Zach.*

Zach plopped into the seat in front of Jake and poked his head around to talk.

"Hey, twerp, having a good flight?"

Just my luck. Five and a half hours to Ireland behind the goon of the eighth grade. "I'd be having a better flight if you'd test the emergency exit."

Zach's eyes narrowed. "Okay, Spanky, you'll pay for that with your leg room." He stuffed his duffle under his own seat until it infringed on Jake's space. "Oh, wait, you're only three feet tall, so my bag won't bother you." Zach chuckled and turned back around to watch a movie on his LCD television screen.

Instinctively, Jake stretched his legs to see if he could reach the duffle with his feet. Shorter than the average student, he felt like a dwarf compared to Zach's football-player physique. He glanced at Zach's seatmate, Julie. *Why doesn't she ever see this?*

Jake's heart pinched as Julie adjusted her position to rest her head on Zach's shoulder. Her blonde hair lay draped between the seats, its strong berry scent sending a slight tingle through Jake's body.

Jake and Julie had grown up together. They'd been friends from hide-and-seek to Guitar Hero, which made it the ultimate blow when she started going out with Zach. *Why can't she see him for the jerk he is?* Jake kicked Zach's bag out of anger. *Good thing no one's sitting next to me.* Then, grinning, he bent forward and slowly opened the zipper.

The first thing he found was a stack of papers. A cover sheet said "The Visitors, by Zachary Maguire." Laughing inwardly at his good fortune, Jake tucked the manuscript into the seat pocket in front of him for future retrieval. *Never pass up good blackmail material.*

Next, he found Zach's security-compliant bag of liquids. *Jackpot! All that bragging about being the only eighth-grader to shave is going to haunt him.* He pulled out the travel-sized can of shaving cream and some dental floss and then pried the tab off his empty soda can.

He knew Julie wouldn't approve of what he was about to do. Like a referee who flags the guy returning a punch, she had a knack for seeing only Jake's retaliations and not Zach's instigating offenses.

After jamming the metal tab into the tight gap behind the button, he gingerly pulled forward on the makeshift lever. Mint-scented goo dribbled out. *Perfect.* Next, he strategically placed a couple of airline blankets inside the duffle to hold the shaving cream can up toward the opening of the bag. He zipped it closed as far as he could, leaving just a little access for his fingers. Using a fisherman's knot, he tied the floss to the metal tab, pulled the slack out, and tied the other end to the zipper.

He bit his lower lip as he pulled the knot tight. *Probably the last time I'll tie that knot, since we no longer have a boat.* The feeling of loss that he experienced on the day his dad sold their sailboat to pay the medical bills had been monumental. He slid the duffle back under the seat and glanced up at the movie. *Seen it.* With his dad laid up, watching movies was about all they could do together now.

*   *   *

Hours later, the pilot announced their descent into Ireland. Jake finished scanning the "Trace Your Heritage" homework instructions and folded them into his backpack. He hadn't wanted to leave New York for the entire summer, but his dad had urged him to go on this school trip, saying it would be good for him to see where their family came from.

Jake tossed his backpack onto the empty seat next to him and peered between the seats as Zach wrapped up the cords of his expensive headphones. *Showtime.* Pretending to sleep, Jake watched through slits in his eyes as Zach pulled out his bag.

Zach tugged at the zipper. It didn't budge. He grunted, tightened his grip, and yanked again. A greenish geyser of minty foam erupted from the bag, lathering Zach from head to waist.

"Argh!" Zach's arms flailed as he struggled to wipe the slime from his face. He stopped and blinked several times. Then he stood up, turned, and fixated on Jake.

Uh-oh. At ten thousand feet, options for escape were slim.

An attendant spoke into the intercom. "Sir, please sit down. We're making our descent."

Temporarily thwarted, Zach pointed at Jake before making a fist and smacking it into his other palm.

"Zach!" Julie scolded.

"But look at what he did!" Zach removed the cream from his face with the last dry part of his shirt.

"Well, what did you think he'd do if you put your bag

there? You know he can't resist a practical joke!"

Jake's heart pounded. *She noticed. There is hope.*

"And Jake, you've got to stop with the pranks." Jake looked down, not wanting to gaze into her disapproving blue eyes. She'd once confided to Jake that Zach had some insecurities and issues with his dad, but Jake didn't think that gave him the right to be a bully.

Once the plane landed in Shannon, the group of ten students made their way through customs and baggage claim. They purchased some cookies and drinks at the café and then walked outside into the mid-morning sun to eagerly await their sponsors. Although most of the students would be going to different villages, such as Ballyferriter and Castlegregory, Jake knew that Zach, Julie, and he would be staying in the town of Dingle.

He remembered the glint in Julie's eyes when she talked about her dad pulling strings to keep them all close to each other. *She wants me to be friends with her boyfriend? No way.*

Jake's name was called. He turned to see a man in faded pants and a colorful sweater bounding toward him. The powerful energy in his trim frame was clearly evident.

"*Dia dhuit*, Jake. Gerald O'Connell *is mo ainm*," he said, warmly extending his hand.

Zach stopped dabbing the shaving cream from his clothes. "Whoa, I thought they spoke English here."

"We do." A girl with long red curls and a china-white complexion stepped out from behind the man. "Hello. My name is Maggie O'Connell, and this is my 'da,'" she said with a charming brogue.

Jake recognized her from the photo she'd sent when they exchanged introductory e-mails. He remembered she was fifteen, only a year older than he was.

Mr. O'Connell inclined his head. "Welcome to Ireland."

Not wanting to pass up the opportunity to upstage Zach, Jake said to Maggie, "That was Irish that your dad—uh, *da*—was speaking, right?"

Maggie beamed. "That's impressive. Most Americans would have called it Gaelic."

"My dad drilled me on Irish knowledge. He didn't want me to bring shame on the McGreevy name."

Maggie smiled in appreciation. "Speaking of names, remember you wrote to ask if there were any McGreevys listed in our area? Well, I was able to find a few near Killorglin—just about an hour away."

"*Go raibh maith agat.*" Jake hoped he'd pronounced the Irish translation for "thank you" correctly.

"Nice."

"'Fraid that's all I've learned so far," Jake grinned.

When Julie's and Zach's names were called, two well-dressed couples approached them. Jake noticed that as each person shook Zach's hand, his or her nose twitched, probably trying to figure out where the minty smell was coming from. Jake snickered and Zach mouthed a threat at him.

In the parking lot, the O'Connells led Jake to a beat-up hatchback. Mr. O'Connell pounded on the latch to open it and began loading Jake's bags. As Zach's and Julie's sponsors packed their luggage into their respective luxury cars, Zach called to Jake, "Hey, twerp. Want me to upgrade you to a donkey cart?"

Maggie squinted at Zach, as if to better understand what he'd just said.

Jake turned to her. "What's Irish for *caveman?*"

She giggled, mischief sparkling in her eyes. "Try *fear pluaise.*"

"Catch you later, *fear pluaise!*"

All the sponsors laughed. And when Zach's face deepened

to a dark shade of red, Jake could barely conceal his pleasure. *I am definitely going to like it here.*

The car's exterior may have been dilapidated, but its engine fired right up. Jake struggled to keep his stomach steady as Mr. O'Connell sped along the highway for the two-and-a-half-hour trip south. Their lively conversation made the time fly. It didn't take long for Jake to get used to their accents, but much to his embarrassment, a few times he found himself unconsciously mimicking their inflections.

"When we get home, you can call your mum and da and tell them you're here," Maggie said.

Jake stared out the passenger window. "Just my dad. My mom died when I was young."

Maggie twisted in her seat to reach out and touch his arm, hesitated, and then put her hand back by her side. *"Tá brón orainn.* I mean, I'm so sorry."

"So this is your first time in Ireland, right, Jake?" Mr. O'Connell said, gently changing the subject.

"Yes. My dad and I have sailed to a few places on our schooner, but we've never made it *this* far."

"Where have you been?" Maggie asked.

"Caribbean mostly. The sea down there is amazing."

"I'll bet. Well, my da and the other sponsors thought you might enjoy seeing a bit of scenery before settling in. We're now on Slea Head Drive. Very soon you'll be able to get your first glimpse of Blasket Sound, okay?"

"Of course." Jake inched forward in his seat for a better view.

As they rounded the next corner, Maggie stretched her arm out the window and said, "Welcome to Dingle."

Jake's jaw dropped as the infinite ocean unfolded before him. Soaring cliffs hugged the coastline to stand guard over white-capped waves racing toward the shore like wild horses.

"It's awesome," Jake said, hoping he didn't sound too corny.

"The *National Geographic Traveller* guidebook proclaimed it 'the most beautiful place on earth,'" Maggie added with pride.

"I can see why."

Thankfully, Mr. O'Connell slowed down a bit to make the curvy ride more enjoyable. Jake glanced back and saw that Zach's and Julie's sponsors were managing to keep pace with Mr. O'Connell. After twenty minutes, everyone pulled into a small parking lot on the western tip of the peninsula.

Several families were gathered at the overlook, all taking pictures of the breathtaking view. The sight of the water overwhelmed Jake, and he swallowed hard, suppressing memories of his father's sailboat and better days. Maggie guided the group to the best vantage point. Unlike some of the spectacular cliffs they had passed on the way, this section of the peninsula was only fifteen feet above the ocean. The water appeared calm, but Jake recalled his dad's many lectures on strong currents and sudden waves.

He looked around at the other tourists and caught sight of a toddler dressed in a thick pink sweater and matching pants. She tottered after a butterfly, swinging her arms in an attempt to catch it. The insect fluttered away from the throngs of people, toward the edge of the cliff, with the child still in pursuit.

Jake swiveled his head around. *Nobody is paying attention to her.* He took off toward the girl, screaming for somebody to stop her, but before anyone could move, the child vanished over the edge. At full speed, Jake shed his shoes and plunged off the cliff.

Chapter 2

Jake slammed into the cold water. His feet stung from the impact and the salty sea burned in his nose and throat. Bobbing to the surface, he scanned the area. *Where is she?* He sucked in a big breath and submerged again. The swirling action of the water pulled dirt from the ocean floor, rendering his sight useless. Using his arms like antennae, he felt everywhere for the girl, frantic.

His lungs seared with pain, forcing him to the surface. He caught a glimpse of people working their way down a sharp trail to a small beach. A woman was screaming so loudly she was drowning out the sounds of the ocean, further fueling the adrenaline already pumping through Jake's veins. Plunging again, he kicked his legs, counting in his mind as he swam further into the abyss. Jake knew he could hold his breath for a long time, but under stress like this, he wasn't sure how much longer he could manage. The seconds ticked by without mercy.

… Eight … nine … ten …

On the scuba-diving trips he'd taken with his father, he'd learned to gauge his distance underwater. He figured he was about fifteen or twenty feet deep.

… Twelve … thirteen … fourteen …

His chest tightened. *No!* Resisting the fatal instinct to breathe, he made a final sweep through the water with his hands.

Got her! He wrapped his fingers around the tiny arm of the toddler. Energized by his prize, he pushed off a boulder and struggled toward the surface. With the limp weight of the toddler dragging him down, he felt as though he were swimming through wet cement. The sunlight drew closer and he gave a final violent kick.

A thunderous cheer erupted from the shore when he emerged holding the child. The color had drained from her face, and he was terrified he was too late. Seconds later, she coughed up some water and cried. *What a wonderful sound.*

As the waves carried him in, he spotted a jagged outcropping of rock. Desperate to rest for a moment, he hugged the girl to him. "Everything's going to be okay," he assured her as he clambered up onto a small shelf, limbs aching and muscles cramping. The sharp edges tore at his skin everywhere, but he brushed off the pain, more concerned with catching his breath and getting the girl safely to dry land.

The crowd hollered to him, "Watch out!"

Jake turned just in time to see the mother of all waves towering overhead. Terror gripping him, he held the girl tighter and searched for something to grab. His left hand found a bit of wood jammed into a crack on a ledge.

The water slammed into them, dragging them both under again. The unrelenting force tumbled them end over end, like socks in a dryer, but Jake didn't lose his hold on the child. Finally, the rolling ceased.

Which way is up?

Just as he began to panic, he felt the grip of strong hands pulling him and the girl onto the shore. Safe at last, Jake collapsed on the beach.

*   *   *

Maggie's voice sliced through the fog in his mind. "Jake! Are you all right?"

Opening his eyes a little, he managed to lift his head from the sand. "I think so," he muttered, and spat out the taste of bitter salt water.

Zach appeared beside Maggie, his eyes shining and his mouth agape. "That was unbelievable. Way to go, McGreevy—I thought that wave was going to split you in half!"

Julie gave Zach a hard stare and then knelt by Jake's side and stroked his arm. "I can't believe you did that," she said, her voice tinged with admiration.

The sensation of her delicate skin touching his elicited a shiver. He temporarily forgot the cuts and massive bruises that were already forming and propped himself into a sitting position.

Mr. O'Connell led the child's parents to Jake and introduced them. The mother almost squeezed the remaining life out of him before leaving to take her daughter to the clinic.

"You're freezing, lad!" Mr. O'Connell said, noticing Jake's chattering teeth. He pivoted and sprinted up the steep bank, calling back over his shoulder, "I'll bring you a blanket from the car."

Zach poked at the piece of wood that Jake was still clutching. "What's that?"

Jake scrutinized the object. It was a small wooden box. "I have no idea. It was jammed in the rock out there."

Zach reached for it and Jake had no energy to put up a fight. The object was covered with sand, moss, and barnacles, and Zach's face scrunched up as he flipped it over in his hands. Julie and Maggie huddled closer to the boys to get a better look.

Remnants of a dark varnish still stained the weather-beaten wood. Maggie leaned closer and rubbed a finger across it. "It's old. I wonder how long it's been in the water."

Jake pointed out some italic letters engraved on the top. "It has initials carved into it ... S.M.R."

"How do you open it?" Zach said impatiently.

"Here, let me." Jake reached for the box, but Zach pulled it away.

Julie twisted Zach's ear. "Give him his box."

Zach released it grudgingly, and Jake scraped at the sand in the seam of the wood with his fingernail. "Must be fused shut or something." He removed his belt and used the thin buckle to pry open the lid. A small object dropped to the sand.

Julie picked it up and held it for the others to see. The heavily tarnished object was in the shape of a flower with a small red ruby still visible at the center. "I think it's a pendant."

"Hey, there's something else in there." Zach pointed to the box. The rotted lining was torn away, revealing a flat piece of metal.

Jake gently freed the artifact from the lining. It was thin, two inches wide and four inches long, with a jagged edge similar to a puzzle piece. "There's writing on this, too. Looks like Spanish."

Zach grabbed it out of Jake's hand and studied the metal. With a horrible Spanish accent, he sounded out the words: "*Ciento Pasos Este en las Nubes de Dios.*"

"Thanks, you big ape."

"It means 'one hundred steps in the clouds of God,'" Julie translated.

Jake remembered Julie's nanny from Panama, who had practically raised her and taught her Spanish in the process. "But what's a Spanish artifact doing off the coast of Ireland?"

Maggie motioned toward the rock shelf where Jake had rested. "There are tons of Spanish wrecks around here. After the Spanish Armada was defeated by England in 1588, many of the ships sailed up here, but storms smashed them into the rocks. The Spanish Navy never recovered, and as a result, there was a shift in power—"

"We got it, Miss Encyclopedia," Zach interrupted, rolling his eyes.

Maggie glowered at him.

"Four hundred years ago? Wow," Jake said, turning the amulet over in his hand and ignoring Zach.

"Something like that. Many museums in Ireland display valuable artifacts—"

Mr. O'Connell returned with the blanket and wrapped Jake up in it. "What's this about artifacts?"

"I was telling them about the treasures from sunken Armada ships," Maggie said. "Jake found something that might be from one of them."

Zach twirled the piece of metal in his fingers. "Jake found? Whoa, Bessie. Possession is nine-tenths of the law."

Jake reached for it. "Hey, I found it. It's mine."

Zach stepped toward the ocean and drew back his arm, poised to hurl the artifact into the violent waves. "Another step and I can end this adventure right now."

"Enough. You kids will work together," Mr. O'Connell said. "Tomorrow you can all go to the Dingle museum. They'll help you figure it all out. Now, Maggie, we've got to go meet your mum at the pub."

Zach slapped Jake on the back. "Guess we're partners, twerp," he said, and trudged up the hill. Julie followed, while Maggie helped Jake, who was still spent from his ordeal.

"You know, Maggie," Jake said, clutching her shoulder for support, "I really like Ireland so far, but I didn't expect it to smell so much like mint."

Zach glared back at him.

Chapter 3

The jolting drive toward the town of Dingle forced every one of Jake's muscles to tighten. He gritted his teeth and braced himself against the backseat, trying to avoid another hit to his already bruised ribs.

Mr. O'Connell prepared to round a tight corner, and Jake held his breath and closed his eyes. He pleaded for gravity to do its job and keep the car attached to the road, but he swore it lifted a little on his side before the road straightened out again.

The moment Jake decided it was safe to look, Mr. O'Connell slammed on the brakes, causing the seatbelt to squish Jake's chest.

Mr. O'Connell banged his fist on the steering wheel and shifted the car into park while muttering something unintelligible that was clearly an Irish curse word.

Maggie's cheeks changed from china white to crimson.

Jake murmured, "I can probably translate that on my own."

She cringed, her cheeks darkening even more.

He peered through the windshield, finally able to absorb the scenery surrounding him. To his left, a river of white sheep blocked the car from moving any further. Longer than a football field, the flock ebbed and flowed as one, their loud bleating drowning the sound of the sputtering engine. Jake and his father had spent every weekend in the upstate New York countryside before the accident, but he hadn't witnessed anything like this there.

Dad would love this. He pulled his smartphone from his backpack, rolled down the window, and snapped some pictures. Even though he knew he would have no cell service, he had packed the gadget for photo opportunities such as this. Then he grimaced and pulled his shirt up over his nose. The smell of the sheep was overpowering. "Is there a fence down or something?"

Maggie shook her head, appearing more bored than floored by the stench. "No, these are pasture commons— public lands where livestock can graze."

Jake's neck whiplashed, unprepared for Mr. O'Connell's sudden decision to move forward again. The hatchback zigzagged through the commotion, accompanied by the sounds of Mr. O'Connell's honking and the bleating of the sheep. Between the impromptu swim, the foul-smelling sheep, and his host's wild driving, Jake's stomach was nearing its limit.

After a few minutes, they were free. With a sudden roar of the engine, the car resumed its breakneck pace and didn't stop until it arrived at one of Dingle's most charming pubs.

Maggie twisted in her seat and smiled at Jake, her eyes twinkling with pride. She motioned toward the small tavern. "This is where my mum works. She's one of the managers. She insisted we bring you here when you arrived."

"Okay, great."

Going into a pub? Is that even legal at my age? Cool.

Jake followed Maggie and her dad into the old stone building, aware that his mouth was opening wider with each step. He admired the rough walls, the ancient oak beams, and the tight weave of the thatch roof. Decades of use had polished the surfaces of the heavy wooden tables and chairs to a smooth sheen. To the right was a bar cut from a solid slab of walnut, fifteen feet long, trimmed with ornate knot-work and a brass rail. A few patrons regarded Jake with indifference and returned to their tall pints of ale.

"Oh, he's here — thank goodness!" A tall slim woman ran from behind the counter, aiming for Jake like a heat-seeking missile.

He wondered if this was how the slowest antelope felt, aware of the lion about to tackle it. Before he had time to react, she was squeezing the breath out of him. He gasped for air, unable to speak or inhale. He knew the Irish prided themselves on hospitality, but how many smotherings could a person survive in one day?

"Pleasure to meet you, Mrs. O'Connell," he whispered hoarsely.

Maggie's cheeks flushed, and with a practiced roll of her eyes, she said, "Mum, let him go already."

Mrs. O'Connell released him, and tousled his hair. Her lips pressed into a stern frown as she shook her head. "You're still wet!"

She turned toward the bar, tucking a loose strand of salt-and-pepper hair back into the knot at the nape of her neck. "Bring me some towels and a hot plate," she barked at one of the bartenders. Then she smiled at Jake, pressing the back of her hand to his forehead. "We've heard about your adventure this morning, lad. Story flew through the village faster than an Irishman heading to the pub on St. Paddy's day. Very heroic."

"Thank you, ma'am." Jake watched her warily, hoping she wouldn't give him another squeeze. The bruises from the battering he'd endured in the ocean were beginning to throb.

Mrs. O'Connell turned to her husband, her expression

blistering. "As for *you*," she scolded. "Putting our guest in danger like that. Tsk!"

Mr. O'Connell wisely bowed his head and apologized to his wife, even though he clearly had done nothing wrong.

Maggie grasped Jake's hand and led him toward a table in the far corner, where a waitress placed an unidentifiable dish before him. Corn, potatoes, and meat whirled together on the plate, their heavenly-smelling steam rising to meet his dripping cold nose.

"That's shepherd's pie, an Irish standard," Mrs. O'Connell said. "That'll put you right."

Maggie leaned forward and whispered to Jake, "If you don't like it, that's okay. Many Americans find it too rich—"

Jake held up his hand and took his seat. Having had only a few snacks since dinner on the flight the night before—and after all he'd been through that morning—he wanted nothing more than to eat something rich and hearty. Minutes later, he was scraping his fork across the empty plate.

"That was delicious," he said as he shoveled in the last bite, his belly full and his body warmed by the meal.

"Guess you really are Irish." Mr. O'Connell winked at him.

"I eat mostly frozen dinners and stuff. Nothing home-made like this," Jake said, wiping his mouth with his napkin. The O'Connells beamed, their warm smiles softening the years of hard living etched into their faces.

Jake figured that Zach and Julie were probably in some marble-tiled dining room with cloth napkins and servants, but he didn't need any of that. The kindness radiating from the O'Connells made this a great meal.

Mr. O'Connell excused himself from the table and Mrs. O'Connell shot rapid-fire questions at Jake about life in America.

"Be right back," Maggie exclaimed as she leapt from the booth. Jake swiveled his head and saw an elderly bartender struggling with a huge keg. Jake started to stand.

"Sit down, young man. You've done quite enough today. My Maggie's got it." Mrs. O'Connell tapped the seat of his chair, leaving no room for argument.

Maggie glided across the room with the grace of a cat, reaching the man just as he was about to drop the keg. She put her shoulder under the barrel and hoisted it away from him. Deftly, she maneuvered it into place behind the bar, gave the man a polite smile, and then walked back to the table.

"That was impressive," Jake said.

Maggie blushed. "Thanks. I've been working at a farm before and after school. It's been great exercise."

"I work some too—mostly cleaning up and fixing things for a home security shop around the corner from our apartment."

They continued to talk about their jobs until a waitress arrived with a plate of warm bread pudding. Still hungry, Jake dug in.

I could get used to this.

Chapter 4

A short time later, Jake set down his fork. An empty dish stared up at him, the only reminder of the fine dessert he'd inhaled.

Satisfaction and fatigue coursed through him now, as the combination of a full stomach and jet lag began to take its toll. He held a fist up to his mouth to mask a yawn and fought to keep his eyelids from drooping.

Mrs. O'Connell hustled about the pub, whistling and wiping the tables in time to the Irish folk music floating in from the kitchen. She caught her daughter's eye and gave her a brief nod.

Maggie made a show of checking her watch. "Jake, my mum and I need to shut the kitchen. But you've had a really long day, so my da can bring you home now and come back for us later."

Mrs. O'Connell tossed the dishrag into the sink behind the bar. She bustled into the dining area, lifted a chair, and placed it upside-down onto the tabletop.

Exhausted as Jake was, he felt it would be rude to leave them to do all the work. Dozens of chairs remained, and most of them still needed wiping down. He rose and grabbed a chair, hoisting it onto the table, just as Mrs. O'Connell had. "Doesn't make much sense for your dad to do that. Why don't I stay and help?"

Mrs. O'Connell ripped the chair from Jake's hands. "Certainly not."

Jake couldn't help but notice the deep furrow in her brow. *Proud people.*

"No, really. I want to help. And besides, moving would do me good."

Mrs. O'Connell's scowl softened into an approving smile. "All right, sweetheart. But you leave the heavy lifting to me."

Jake followed her into the supply room and returned with an armful of cleaning supplies. He spent the next hour helping Maggie clean and mop the floor. Mr. O'Connell finished the tables, while Mrs. O'Connell shouted orders and inspected their workmanship. She wouldn't let any of them leave until the place gleamed and the odors of food, sweat, and spilled beer were eradicated.

When Mrs. O'Connell's exacting standards were finally met, Jake and Maggie gathered up his belongings and headed toward the tiny hatchback. As Jake scrunched into the back, Maggie implemented a well-practiced contortionist maneuver, pretzeling her long legs next to Jake in the milk crate masquerading as a rear seat.

Jake had a difficult time focusing on anything while Mr. O'Connell whizzed over the darkening cobblestone streets. He wasn't sure if the trip was two or twenty miles. He closed his eyes and focused on keeping his meal down.

Abruptly, the vehicle lurched to a halt. The seatbelt dug into Jake's chest, and he winced against the brief sting before opening his eyes. Being still had never felt so good.

The O'Connells each grabbed one of his bags out of the rear of the car, and Jake caught his first glimpse of their home. Built of large fieldstones, it had a whitewashed exterior and black-trimmed windows. Though small by American standards, it was surrounded by an apple orchard, and the car's headlights illuminated a barn.

Maggie led the way to the front door. The main living area

had a fireplace, a sofa, two chairs covered with faded floral slipcovers, and a small television with a bent antenna. Jake wondered what types of TV shows aired in Dingle.

Mrs. O'Connell switched on the evening news. The main story was about a string of recent museum robberies. Maggie cranked up the volume.

"There are still no clues as to who these criminals are or where they will strike next," the anchor said in an overly dramatic fashion. "Having stolen valuable historical artifacts from six museums and three graveyards on, curiously, only Tuesdays and Thursdays, they've been dubbed the Mid-Week Bandits. As police increase patrols, many museums are hiring extra security, fearful of becoming their next victim."

When the story ended, Maggie clicked off the TV. "Isn't it fascinating?"

Jake had to smile. *She would be shocked by the news in New York City.* He began to respond, but only a yawn emerged from his mouth.

"Best get you off to bed," Maggie said, resisting a yawn herself.

"Great idea." Jake pried himself off the chair, where he could've easily fallen asleep had he not been in the company of strangers.

She led him to a room at the end of the hallway, where Mr. O'Connell had already delivered his luggage. "This was my brother David's room."

Hundreds of photos were pinned to the walls, and dozens of trophies and ribbons littered the dresser. A hefty rugby jersey hung on the wall over the bed.

Wow. This is what a room should be.

Jake recalled his own room in Brooklyn, undecorated since the move from their comfortable brownstone to a tiny two-bedroom apartment near the rehab center where his father now spent most of his days. "Rugby, huh?"

Maggie grinned, the dimples in her cheeks deepening, her eyes sparkling. "David was the best rugby player in Dingle, possibly on the whole peninsula. He even went pro for a short time before he injured his knee."

"Too bad. Well, where is he now?"

"In Dublin. He works in an auto repair shop and attends classes at night. He's going to operate his own garage one day." Maggie opened the closet door and slid her brother's remaining clothes to one side.

Jake noted how Maggie had said *going to,* the confidence in and love for her brother apparent. All the pictures in the room showed at least one of the O'Connells with David, beaming with pride. A familiar pang of loneliness speared Jake's heart.

One non-sports-related picture caught his attention, and he picked it up. It was a photo of Maggie, dressed in a short colorful dress, with white stockings and black shoes. She held a giant trophy and was among a group of girls her age. "What's this?"

Maggie snatched the picture from his hands and put it into a drawer. "I used to dance in a troupe. That was taken the night we won the annual Irish dance competition."

Jake detected a slight pang of remorse and frowned. "You were the lead, right?"

Her brow creased and she crossed her arms. "How do you figure?"

"I think in every culture, the person holding the trophy is the lead." He grinned, surprised by her shyness.

Bright pink splotches broke out across her skin, from neck to forehead. She glanced sideways. "Oh."

Fueled by their new connection, he blurted, "I love Irish music. It sounds dorky coming from an American kid, but I don't care. I play the violin in our school's orchestra and we once played the song 'Riverdance.' It was great."

She picked up her head and grinned. "I bet you were first chair, weren't you?"

"How do you figure?"

Maggie pointed at Jake's hard fingertips. "I think in every culture, whoever has calluses on his hands spends a lot of time doing the same thing. For you, it must be practicing the violin. Sorry, I noticed them when you were mopping."

Jake impulsively rubbed his thumb along his fingertips. He'd never paid attention to them before now. "So why'd you stop dancing?"

Maggie checked the hallway and then replied in a hushed tone. "My da lost his job. I've been helping at the pub and doing odd jobs in the village for extra money. Bless the work."

"Oh. I read that most small towns have been hurting and that finding work is really difficult."

Maggie nodded and smiled gratefully.

Mrs. O'Connell came into the room carrying a large blanket. "Here you go, love. Summer nights can be quite chilly here."

"Thank you."

Jake spread the blanket on top of the bed, and Mrs. O'Connell gave him another bear hug. "We're thrilled to have you with us. We are, lad."

Jake rubbed his hand along the thick plush blanket. *I bet this is their best one.* "Thank you. I feel very welcome."

"*Oíche mhaith*," Mrs. O'Connell said as she left the room.

Jake looked expectantly at Maggie. "Translate?"

"Good night," she grinned.

"Oh. Well, *oíche mhaith*, then."

Maggie closed the door to his room. Jake sat down on the bed. The happy family pictures needled him—a wall full of reminders of the life he used to have. He pressed a button on his two-time-zone watch. *Only the middle of the afternoon in New York. I'll call Dad tomorrow.*

He decided to get into bed before he started feeling too sorry for himself.

Chapter 5

Jake rolled under the covers and squinted against the morning sun. He read his watch and bolted upright.

9:30 AM. I haven't slept that long since …

Jake's brain shut down the thought, avoiding the memory of that dreadful day. He sat up in the bed, letting the fog of sleep clear from his mind. A twinge of guilt shot through his chest.

Should have tried to reach Dad last night. I'd better send an e-mail before breakfast.

He stared longingly at his pillow, the pastel floral print beckoning him like a siren to return to sleep. *Is it the jet lag, or was Dad right … I'm worn out from trying to be the man of the house?*

He forced himself to get dressed.

When he entered the kitchen, Maggie jumped up from her chair and set down a bowl of oats and milk for Jake. The meager breakfast wasn't long on flavor, but the hospital food he'd eaten with his dad had conditioned him to stomach the blandest of meals.

"I take it you've been up for a while," he said.

She nodded, tucking a stray curl behind her ear. "A farmer down the road pays me to help feed his pigs a couple of days a week."

"Bless the work."

"You catch on quick. Pretty soon you'll be wearing a kilt like a real Irishman."

Jake suppressed a laugh. *I'm not dressing in a skirt while Zach's around, that's for sure.*

Maggie tilted her chin back and drained the remaining milk from her bowl.

Jake put down his spoon and looked at her closely for the first time. It wasn't just her vibrant red hair or her creamy complexion. What drew Jake in the most were her eyes. Their deep emerald green was clear enough to see his reflection in. He wasn't sure if it was the hectic travel or the poor lighting in the pub yesterday, but he was surprised that he hadn't noticed how pretty she was before.

Her nose scrunched. "Is something wrong?"

"Sorry! I drifted off there. Must be jet lag." His cheeks baked under her gaze.

"We should probably get going soon. The museum will open at ten and it will take a little while to ride there. You should be able to use my brother's bike."

Jake followed Maggie on a small brick path through the orchard to the barn. The crackling paint seemed to be the only thing holding the weathered slats of wood together.

Maggie leaned into the old door and it creaked open to reveal an enormous collection of junk: tools, ladders, old furniture, and other items littered the dirt floor.

Probably spiders, mice, and bats in here, too.

"Here." Maggie pointed to two bikes leaning against the wall. She grabbed her ladies' bike, and Jake wheeled out her brother's. He swung his leg over the bar and realized the seat was far too high for him.

Maggie walked to the workbench, where tools hung on pegs on the wall. "Well, we might have some useful tools here. I don't know what you would need ..."

"That's okay." Jake opened his backpack and found his well-worn Leatherman multi-tool, the world's greatest invention. With even more attachments and gadgets than a Swiss Army knife, it came in handy almost daily. His dad had carried it everywhere, even when he went to business meetings in a suit.

Jake reflexively rubbed the engraving of his dad's initials with his fingertips. Then, with a few quick adjustments, he moved the seat to the optimal height and worked on tightening the bolts.

"That's a pretty neat tool," Maggie said.

"My dad's. He was always disassembling things and putting them back together. I don't go anywhere without it."

"*Was?* He doesn't use it anymore?"

Jake twisted the bolt one last time, taking a moment to collect the familiar flurry of feelings before he stood up. "He was in an accident. He was confined to a hospital bed in our apartment for a long time, but now he can wheel back and forth to rehab on his own."

Maggie touched Jake's arm. "How awful. Is he getting better?"

Jake put the Leatherman back into his pack and moved out of her reach, his stomach clenching. He tried to strip the emotion from his voice. "He can't move his legs. We bought him an electric wheelchair so he can be more independent. Never mind. Let's go, okay?"

Maggie hesitated and then nodded and led Jake out to the road. He fought to keep the bike straight on the bumpy cobblestone roads.

As they rode, Jake stole glances at the old houses. *Chimneys on both sides, nonpaired windows, and decorative tooth-like moldings.* "These are Georgian-style homes, right?" he called to Maggie.

She grinned. "Yes! They were built between 1720 and 1840. Where did you learn about Georgian buildings?"

"My dad's an architect. He used to quiz me when we traveled. He loves old houses."

She snorted and pedaled harder. "Old? I wish I could show you Ashford Castle. It's beautiful and was built in 1228. But it's far from here."

Jake laughed. "I guess age is relative. In the States, except for some Pueblo stuff out west and buildings in Puerto Rico, nothing we call old dates back to the Middle Ages."

They reached a busier section of town, full of shops and cars and people. Maggie dismounted and began to walk her bike. "Well, actually, the Middle Ages is recent compared to the six thousand years of history right here on the peninsula, but—"

Jake stopped. The activity surrounding him became nonexistent. No Maggie, no cars, no people. Not even air. Just Julie. Straight ahead, peering into a shop window. Alone.

Apparently, she left her ogre at home. Jake doubled his pace, checking the sidewalk as he approached her for any signs of Zach. "Hey, Julie!"

She turned around, and his pulse accelerated when her eyes locked with his. "Hi, Jake. Hi, Maggie."

Jake suddenly realized from Maggie's expression that he'd cut her off. "Um—the O'Connells have a really nice house, and I ... I slept the best I have in a long time," he said, fumbling to make up for his mistake.

"Lucky you," Julie replied. "I was so excited about finding that pendant yesterday, I didn't sleep a wink."

"Yeah. A rusty piece of metal and a blob of tarnish. I'm still tingling." Zach materialized from nowhere and wedged himself between Maggie and Julie, draping his arms over both girls' shoulders. Maggie's eyes flared as she shrugged off Zach's arm. "*Sracadh.*"

What a jerk. "You don't have to go with us, you know," Jake said.

30

Zach's grin widened. "And let you explore Ireland alone with these two beautiful women? Not a chance, twerp."

Julie huddled closer to Zach, allowing his arms to enfold her even tighter.

Jake turned to Maggie, unable to bear any more of Julie and Zach's touching. "We should get to the museum. Which way, Maggie?"

Maggie pointed down the street. "This way."

Chapter 6

Zach and Julie mounted their bikes, which had been stashed on a nearby rack. Zach's was a brand-new twenty-one-speed mountain bike, which would've taken Jake months to save up for. *It figures.*

Jake squinted at his rusty steed and tried to kick off some of the dirt caked on the wheels. He glanced at Maggie, who frowned at him. *Crud. I've offended her again.*

She led the way and the group pedaled the few miles to the museum. Fueled by his excitement at the possibility of having found treasure, Jake practically flew through the door, nearly knocking off the small bell hanging on the knob.

A silver-haired man wearing a ragged cardigan and frayed trousers poked his head around the counter. "What's the rush, lad?"

"Um, hi, sorry," Jake said. "We have some questions ..."

"We found something on the beach," Julie announced. "We believe it might be a Spanish antique."

The man paused for a moment. "Well, then. I'm Shamus, the museum curator. Let's have a peek."

Maggie walked up next to Jake and set the box on the counter. "We were at Blasket Sound, and we found this."

Shamus rubbed his fingers along the edge of the wooden box. Jake watched as his wrinkled hands carefully opened it.

"Hmmm." The man pulled a magnifying glass from under the counter and peered at the rose pendant. "It is old. Not sure it's Spanish, though. What made you think that?"

Jake's heart pounded in his chest. *It has to be something.*

It just has to be. He set the piece of metal on the counter. "We found this with it. See the Spanish writing?"

"*Ciento Pasos Este en las Nubes de Dios,*" Shamus read without hesitation. "Well, it could be from a Spanish ship."

"That's what we thought—from the Spanish Armada!" Maggie's voice squeaked and Jake watched her cheeks get red.

"Oh, I don't know about that, lassie. Old for sure, but not four hundred years."

The letdown tore at Jake's chest. He wanted to shout, but he contained himself. "Why not?"

"This is an old country, lad, and you can dig up all sorts of bits and bobs … but most of it's just tinkers' tin. Tell you what. Why don't you kids leave these with me and I'll see what I can find out."

Jake picked up the box and the artifacts. "Thank you, but I think we'll keep working on it ourselves. We'll be back later if we don't find anything."

Shamus nodded. "Okay, I'll be here." A kettle whistled nearby. "That's my tea. You children have a good day," he said as he turned toward the back room.

Jake arranged the items in his backpack as the kids stepped outside. "I can't believe these aren't something special. Julie, do you have an international data plan on your smartphone?"

"Sure, I do. Here." Julie handed Jake her phone.

The others crowded around as Jake brought up the Internet. "Not sure why we didn't do this in the first place." He typed "Spanish Armada, Blasket Sound, S.M.R." into the search box. "Here's something … SantaMariaDeLaRosa. com." Jake clicked on the link, his pulse racing again. *I don't think I can take this emotional roller coaster much longer.* The page loaded and he read the text out loud.

"'Santa Maria de la Rosa. Saint Mary of the Rose. It sank in 1588 in Blasket Sound.'"

"Blasket Sound. That has to be it!" Julie cried.

"There's more. 'An argument broke out between the crew and the Captain over missing treasure. During the brawl, the navigator got distracted and the ship drifted into the breakers. A young boy was the only survivor and he told rescuers of the great debts the Captain had amassed in Spain. The crew had been certain he had buried the treasure on the southwest peninsula of the Irish coast with the intent to return later and claim it as his own.'"

"If that's true, then we just found part of his treasure," Julie said, "and probably a clue to where the rest is as well."

"But why didn't Shamus tell us that?" Maggie interjected.

"Nobody knows anything anymore," Zach snorted. "Why learn stuff from old folks when you can find out what you need on the Internet? I bet gramps back there doesn't even have a computer."

"That's probably true," Jake said, surprised to find himself agreeing with Zach. "I bet Shamus isn't up to date on his knowledge."

Maggie looked at her watch. "Well, we'll have to research this more, but right now I've got some chores to do."

"And I have to go to that tourist store we passed," said Julie. "I need another memory card for my camera—mine's not working right."

"Well, knock yourself out," Zach groaned. "I gotta get some fish and chips or whatever people eat around here. I'm starved."

Narcissistic jerk. "I'll go with you, Julie." Jake hoped his voice didn't sound too desperate. "It's pretty easy to find my way back to the O'Connells."

Chapter 7

Jake and Julie wandered around the tourist shop, scanning the assorted trinkets and useless plastic objects. Key chains featuring local landmarks lined the shelves, along with cheap sweatshirts that would undoubtedly pill after the first wash and chocolate candy in the shape of the local indigenous animal poop.

Nothing piqued Jake's interest. Having visited hundreds of tourist shops on travels with his father, he'd always marveled at how every one in every country sold the same junk.

Julie found the memory card she wanted and went to the register, where she handed over the credit card she kept tucked in her leather cell phone case. Customers like Julie had unlimited lines of credit, something shop owners never failed to recognize. Jake wasn't surprised. Julie's father was a partner at a prestigious law firm and worked around the clock. Jake had been to Julie's house a lot but had only met her father twice.

After she paid, they walked their bikes to the end of the block where there was a small grocery store with crates of fruit stacked on the sidewalk near the entrance. Suddenly, the sun disappeared behind a gigantic man who stepped out of the shadows of the building. He wore dark jeans and a flannel shirt that was covered in stains. He looked as if he hadn't shaved or combed his hair in days.

The man dangled two beat-up tickets inches from Jake's

nose. His fingers reeked of motor oil and stale cigarette smoke. "How d'ye do? Me name's Malic. How'd the two of ye like to see a magic show?"

Jake and Julie were no strangers to street swindlers. Jake smirked, curious to learn whether Irish cons were any different from those back home. "Magic, huh?"

Malic jabbed his thumb over his shoulder to a slight gap between two buildings and winked. "It's in a small shop on the other side of this alley, here. But it starts soon, so ye'd best hightail it."

The huge man took a step toward the kids, and alarm raced through Jake's body. He reached for Julie's hand and noticed her fingers were icy and trembling. "We do like magic, but we have to …"

"What, kid?" Malic said, his appearance darkening. He stepped even closer and coughed, overcome by wheezing.

Jake glanced sideways at Julie, who gave him a little wink.

"Now!" Jake said.

Julie delivered a sharp kick to the man's shins and took off.

Malic's face curled in on itself, and he howled like a wounded animal, bending his knee to cradle his leg and hopping to keep his balance.

As Julie jumped onto her bike, Jake took hold of an apple crate and hurled it, sending the fruit skittering. Malic lunged for Jake, but the brute stumbled over the fruity obstacle course and crashed to the ground.

Jake sped after Julie on his rickety bike, his heart beating like crazy. She bunny-hopped a tall curb and kept pedaling, as if she hadn't just done a terrific Evil Knievel impression. His lips spread into a grin. *Not your typical cheerleader.*

David's old bike was too heavy for Jake, and it didn't quite clear the curb. The rear tire banged hard against the concrete.

Steadying himself, Jake stole a glance backward. Malic was nowhere to be seen.

"I think we're ... in the clear ... now," Jake panted.

"Can you believe he tried the old *magic show across the alley* lure?" Julie shouted back, barely winded.

Jake's muscles were on fire, trying to keep up. Sweat dripped down his face and neck. "Yeah, we should just wear T-shirts that say 'New Yorkers! Muggers, go elsewhere.'"

Julie released an exultant laugh and rounded the corner. They found the quiet road to her sponsors' home and pedaled side by side at an easier pace the rest of the way. When they arrived, Jake walked Julie to the door, his hands stuffed in his pockets. "I had fun today."

"Me, too. What does all this treasure talk mean?" she asked.

"I have no idea. But I'm excited to solve the mystery with you." The cold wind nipped at his ears, and he noticed that Julie had goose bumps on her arms, yet it seemed as if she were expecting him to say something more.

After a few awkward seconds, he said, "Well, I guess you'd better go inside so you don't freeze."

She smiled and vanished into the house.

Nice going. You could have kissed her right there, and then she'd have realized she made a mistake in choosing Zach. You'll never get a better opportunity and you just blew it.

Jake grumbled at his cowardice the entire ride back to Maggie's.

* * *

As he entered the kitchen, his nose twitched at an enticing smell. After all the energy he'd expended biking, he'd worked up a tremendous appetite.

Maggie was ladling Irish stew from a pot on the stove into two bowls. "It's just you and me for dinner tonight."

"Oh, why is that?"

"My mum is working, and since it's Tuesday, my da is out."

"What does he do on Tuesday nights?"

She shook her head. "Dunno. He's just … out on Tuesdays and Thursdays. Mum and I gave up asking a while ago."

Jake sat at the table across from Maggie, digging into his stew and telling her about Julie's and his run-in with the local would-be mugger. He devoured every bite of the meat-and-potato meal, savoring the pleasant change from dinners at home.

Home, he thought for a moment. He still lived with his dad, but was it really a home? They barely talked anymore. They had once been constantly active outdoors—sailing, riding horses, all kinds of sports—and now they flipped coins over whether to watch crime shows or sports.

"What are you daydreaming about?" Maggie asked.

Jake coughed, trying to clear any sadness that might remain in his voice. "Just trying to decipher the Spanish clue on that piece of metal."

"A hundred steps in the clouds of God. Let's break it down," she said.

"Good idea. *Steps* seems fairly straightforward. What about *clouds of God?*"

Maggie leaned back in her chair and stared at the ceiling. "Well, the God portion could refer to a church, right?"

"Sure. But what are the clouds?" Jake asked.

"Clouds … clouds. What's special about clouds?"

"They're white?"

"A white church!" They spoke in unison.

Jake tore away from the table and retrieved an Irish travel book from his backpack.

"Is there anything you don't keep in your backpack?" Maggie asked.

"Spanish treasure," Jake joked, skimming the travel book. "Okay, let's assume the Web site was right and the captain was familiar with this peninsula. There are dozens of churches in the area."

"But how many existed in the 1500s?"

Jake combed through the descriptions. "Six, total. Let's shorten the list by checking the colors ..."

Maggie moved next to Jake and traced a route on the map with her finger. "Maybe not. The paint colors might have changed since then, you know? Anyway, it shouldn't be too difficult a bike ride. We can probably see them all in one day."

He jumped toward the phone. "Sounds good. Let's call Julie."

"What about Zach?" Maggie said.

Jake's shoulders slumped. "Julie can call him."

Chapter 8

Jake gripped the handle on the door to the small stone church. The parking area was empty and he wondered if they would even be able to get inside.

He pushed against it, and the door creaked, signaling its age as it swung open. The stone-floored sanctuary was a marvel of craftsmanship. Elaborate stained-glass windows depicting numerous scenes from the Bible provided the only source of light.

The room was small by modern church standards, with only ten rows of old wooden pews. At the front of the church, a simple pulpit stood next to a large iron cross.

Jake stared up at the ceiling, which was exquisitely painted with cherubs, prophets, and animals. "Wow."

Julie aimed her camera at the ceiling and snapped a photo. "This picture won't do it justice, but I want to remember how pretty it is."

Zach lumbered behind the lectern. His voice boomed inside the small sanctuary. "Lord, please forgive Jake for being such a toolbox."

"Zach!" Julie said.

"Yeah, that wasn't funny the first five times today," Maggie echoed.

Jake wandered to the side of the church where a spiral staircase led to a small balcony. "Only twenty steps here. What about the size of the sanctuary?"

Maggie paced the distance from the entrance to the pulpit and flopped down in one of the pews. "Nowhere near a hundred steps. We've visited all six churches and not one of them has either a hundred stairs or is a hundred steps across. Maybe we were wrong about the church."

"Gee, what gives you that idea?" Zach said.

"Why don't you see if holy water will remove your feral animal smell?" Jake retorted.

Zach narrowed his eyes and began walking toward him but froze when the sound of a car door slamming resonated throughout the sanctuary.

"Hide!" Maggie said.

Jake and Maggie stooped behind the pulpit, while Julie and Zach hid under a row of pews. The heavy door creaked open and footsteps bounced off the stone walls.

"This is the last one, and there ain't no way there's a hundred steps here," a gruff voice called.

Jake tried to peek around the pulpit, but Maggie yanked him back out of sight.

"The boss is going to be mad," another voice growled.

"Well, the *boss* didn't spend the day wandering the countryside, rooting about in churches. Come on. These places give me the willies."

Jake tensed his fists until the voices receded. He and Maggie waited to emerge until they heard the car drive off.

"What was that about?" Julie asked, as she reappeared with Zach.

"Seems we're not the only ones searching for the treasure," Maggie replied.

Jake peered through one of the windows, attempting to catch a glimpse of the trespassers. "Anybody get a good view of them?"

"I saw one. He was tall and skinny with wire-rimmed

glasses and a pointy nose," Julie said.

Jake peeked out the door to see if the car had left. He frowned. "Did anyone else think one of those voices sounded familiar?"

"I did," Julie said.

Zach shrugged, nonchalant as usual. "Guys with Irish accents—what a surprise. Let's get out of here. I want some ice cream."

"Always focused on your stomach, huh, Neanderthal?" Jake said.

"Hey, these guns don't run on air." Zach flexed his biceps and rotated his fists side to side to show off the different ways his muscles twitched.

Jake sighed, hoping to hide the jealousy bubbling up inside.

* * *

The gang biked to a nearby ice cream shop overlooking the ocean. Maggie dismounted and headed for some picnic tables. "I'm not hungry right now. I'll save us a table."

"Not hungry?" Zach said with disbelief. "We've been riding all day and you didn't even have a snack at the food stand when we stopped for lunch."

Maggie ignored him and continued toward an empty table.

A few minutes later, Jake appeared carrying two ice cream cones to the table. "I ordered swirl but they gave me chocolate by accident," he said, hoping his plan would work. "Instead of throwing it away, I thought I'd see if anybody else wanted it. Maggie?"

She appeared stunned for a moment. Then her gaze softened into a smile. "Now that I've rested, I guess I am kind of hungry."

Jake handed the cone to her, his fingers accidentally

brushing hers. Little prickles played on his skin where they'd touched.

Maggie waited until Julie and Zach weren't paying attention and then leaned into Jake. "Thanks," she whispered in his ear.

He nodded and bit into his cone, hiding the satisfied smile on his lips.

Julie finished her cone and turned to Maggie, pointing. "Those rocks out there in the ocean look so mysterious. Do you know anything about them?"

Jake followed her finger and saw two clusters of sharp white rock jutting out of the water several miles away.

"Oh, those are the Skellig Islands. There's an old monastery on top of the bigger one, Skellig Michael." Maggie took another bite of her cone.

Zach's smug grin met her reply. "A monastery. I can just see a bunch of bald-headed guys sitting around worshipping God on that pile of clouds out there."

Jake's heart leapt. "That's it!" *Of course it would be Zach who made the connection.* Jake couldn't contain his excitement. He dug into his backpack and pulled out his already well-worn guidebook. He thumbed through the pages. "'Skellig Michael dates back to around the seventh century. Each year, thousands of tourists walk up the six hundred stone steps from the shore to view the remnants of an austere monastic life that existed for about six hundred years.'"

Julie stood and walked to the edge of the picnic area. "Hundreds of steps ... that must be it! Maybe the next clue is on the hundredth step."

Maggie and Jake shushed her, motioning to the nearby patrons.

"What times do the tours run?" Julie whispered to Maggie.

"I don't know. I've lived here all my life but I've never been across."

Jake dug into the book. "Boats leave each hour from 9:00 AM to 3:00 PM." He slammed the book shut. "Tomorrow, we find the treasure."

He stared at the island. *And when I find it, I'll buy Dad's sailboat back. I'll manage the sails while Dad sits and steers, and everything will be back to normal.*

Chapter 9

Jake woke early the next morning and was unable to go back to sleep. He willed the clock to move faster toward the opening time of Skellig Michael.

He found the manuscript he'd liberated from Zach's backpack. With the excitement surrounding the treasure hunt, he'd forgotten all about it. After reading several pages, he found himself leaning forward in bed. *This is good. Not what you'd expect from a pigskin-carrying caveman like Zach.*

He read on, disappointed when the story stopped mid-sentence on the fiftieth page. *I must have only stolen the first part.*

Jake heard Maggie return from her early morning chores and go into the bathroom to shower. He'd offered to help with the chores and she had refused, saying her parents would freak.

He decided to pack his gear and pulled one of his most prized possessions from the suitcase. It was a pen-sized fiber-optic camera, a damaged item returned to the security shop by an angry customer. Jake had tinkered with it for two months before he was able to repair it. Then he'd created an adapter so it interfaced with his smartphone.

He tested all the connections and, satisfied that it had survived the plane ride, went into the hallway to meet Maggie. The toe of his sneaker caught in a roll in the carpet, and the floor rushed up to meet his face.

Dazed, he shook his head and realized the camera had

fallen out of his hand. "Shoot," he said, his heart sinking at the thought of all the time and work he'd invested going to waste.

He picked it up and flipped the power switch with his thumb. Relief flooded over him as the lights flickered on and the image of the bathroom door showed on the screen. Just as he was about to turn it off, the bathroom door opened, and Maggie's legs appeared on the display.

"Oh, you scared me!" Maggie peered at Jake, kneeling on the floor. She was wrapped in a towel and her long wet hair dripped water on the floor.

Jake's cheeks flushed with heat. *Please don't make a big deal. Please don't make a big deal.* He smiled up at her and waved.

"What do you have there?" She crouched next to Jake. "A *camera?* Jake McGreevy, were you peeking through the keyhole?"

"No! I … I fell and it just switched on," he stammered, his shaking hands barely able to hold the phone.

"Sure it did." Maggie gave him a little wink that flooded him with confusion. Her tone made Jake think she was angry. But there was a definite twinkle in her eyes.

Girls.

*   *   *

Jake waited with Maggie, Julie, and Zach for the captain of the tour boat to open the gate and allow them to board. He had convinced Maggie to let him pay for her ticket when the others weren't watching.

As they boarded, Jake watched Maggie dash for a seat in the center of the boat. She relaxed visibly when her hands made contact with a life jacket stowed beneath.

"Are you okay?" Jake asked as he sat down beside her.

She leaned toward him and whispered, "I can't swim."

"Can't swim? You live on an island, for crying out loud," Zach bellowed behind them.

"Apparently, a side effect of having no brain is superhuman hearing. Ignore him." Jake squeezed Maggie's hand and then quickly pulled his away.

The boat bounced over the choppy ocean waves toward the magnificent islands, which jutted out of the water like two jagged volcanoes. Jake breathed in the thick ocean air. *Dad was right. It's good to smell the sea again.*

Thousands of sea birds wheeled and squawked overhead as the boat pulled alongside the stone landing of Skellig Michael. Jake gazed up at the outline of the ancient ruins, rising more than seven hundred feet above the water. *Too bad we're not going all the way up.*

They disembarked and waited for the majority of the crowd to start up the rugged stone steps before beginning their ascent. Jake meticulously counted each one by marking off a grid of numbers he had drawn the night before.

As they reached the nineties, his heart began to pound with anticipation. A small twelve-inch square was carved into one of the stones above. *The hundredth step!*

Jake sprinted up the remaining seven stairs, knelt, and traced the block with his hands. "I'll use my Leatherman to clean the dirt from the cracks," he said to Maggie.

He quickly pulled the trusty device from his backpack, and after a few minutes of scraping, the grooves were free of any dirt.

"Someone's coming," Julie hissed, tapping Jake's shoulder.

Jake jumped up and posed with Maggie while Julie snapped a picture. An elderly Japanese couple trudged past them, glaring suspiciously at Jake as they did so. Once they had passed, Zach marched behind them, waving his hands as if to shoo them away.

Julie giggled and the couple turned around. Busted, Zach quickly spun in the other direction and mumbled something inaudible to the others. After a few minutes the couple moved on out of sight.

"Man, I thought they'd never get past us. I bet they set the record for world's slowest stair climb," Zach said.

"Have respect for your elders," Maggie said.

Zach gave a little snarl, but Jake interrupted them. "Guys, we're digging for treasure here. Focus!" He grunted as he tried to pry up the thick stone and wished the other three weren't watching him so intently.

Zach sighed and pushed Jake aside. "Move over. Leave the heavy lifting to the real men." He stood over the stone and tried pulling it up, but despite his larger size, he, too, fought with the rock.

"Pretty manly display, all right," Jake said, not bothering to hide his satisfaction.

"Once I get this rock up, I'm going to smack you with it," Zach groaned, straining to yank up the stone. After a dozen more heaves, the block popped free.

Zach rolled it to one side and the others crowded in to see what was in the hole. A few beetles crawled around inside. Maggie swatted them away with her visitor's pamphlet and then reached in and withdrew a rotted velvet sleeve.

"Is it another puzzle piece?" Jake knew it couldn't already be the treasure. That would be too easy. Nevertheless, part of him hoped they'd already found the riches.

Maggie removed the cover and handed the artifact to Julie, who rubbed away the dirt until she could read the words: "*Cein pasos al sur de ventana de España.*"

"Translate!" the gang chorused.

"It means 'Fifty feet from Spain's window.'"

"'Fifty feet from Spain's window,'" Jake repeated. He

looked at Maggie, hoping she knew what it meant.

"No idea," she said. "We'd better talk about it later. A tour group is returning."

Zach moved the stone back into its place and the kids shuffled downward.

"Why do you think the captain hid the clues?" Julie wondered aloud.

"Well," Maggie said, "carrying around a treasure map would have been a bit obvious, right? So—"

"Oh, who can guess what was in someone's mind more than four hundred years ago?" Zach interrupted. "Maybe the captain was just posing as a Spaniard. Perhaps he was really an Irish adventurer who found himself back home on the peninsula with a shipload of treasure, and then, under cover of darkness, had it secretly transferred—"

"Very funny," Jake said. "Listen, that was fascinating. But I think we should concentrate on our goal of actually *finding* the treasure, don't you?"

When the boat returned to the harbor, they ran for their bikes. Jake had just finished securing the piece of metal in his backpack when a booming voice stopped them in their tracks.

"Hold it there!"

A burly man, wearing knee-high rubber boots and a yellow slicker stood behind them. "I'm the harbormaster. I hear you kids took something off the island."

Julie stepped forward, flashing the harbormaster her most stunning smile. "We sure did."

Jake bit his bottom lip. *What is she doing?*

"We took a lot of pictures. The view is *incredible.*" She lifted her camera and showed him some pictures on its LCD screen.

"That's nice, lassie. I'll just check what's in this backpack." He reached for Jake's ever-present accessory.

Jake crossed his arms, trying to appear tough, although his insides were in turmoil. "Don't you need a warrant?"

"You watch too much TV, lad. Read the poster." The man directed them to a sign on the dock stating that visitors' bags were subject to inspection.

Trapped, Jake unzipped his backpack. The harbormaster sifted through the electronic gear, pulled the piece of metal from the small pouch, and dangled it in front of Jake's nose. "What's this?"

"A shoe horn," Julie said.

Zach coughed to cover a laugh.

"Humph. We'll see about that. It appears to be some sort of artifact. I'll be impounding this." The man grunted and walked away from them.

Once he was out of earshot, Maggie raised an eyebrow at Julie. "A shoe horn?"

"Sorry. It just popped out."

As the harbormaster headed off with their clue toward a small dilapidated building at the end of the pier, Jake felt a mounting cloud of rage.

Zach punted a rock across the street with his shoe, missing a family of tourists by inches. "I can't believe we just got busted by the Gorton's Fisherman."

Chapter 10

Transfixed by the harbormaster's retreating form, Jake cracked his knuckles and began to follow him. Then, with a calm determination, he sped up, running to catch the yellow blob of rain slicker.

So far, he'd traveled across an ocean, jumped off a cliff, and been chased by a street thug. No way would he let a dorky harbormaster stand in the way of reclaiming his dad's boat. Not when he was this close.

Maggie jogged to catch up with him and tried to block his way. "Where are you going?"

"To recover our puzzle piece."

"You can't be serious," she said, crossing her arms. "He could have you sent back home—to *America*, I mean."

Jake met her disbelieving eyes and said, "Only if I'm caught."

Julie and Zach joined them. Julie touched his arm, her expression a mixture of worry and astonishment. "What's going on?"

Maggie glared at Jake and said, "McGreevy here thinks he's going to steal the clue back."

Jake didn't give any of them a chance to argue. He sidestepped Maggie and darted behind the building that the harbormaster had gone into, staying low and in the shadows. Heart racing, he crept alongside the stone exterior until he came to a window and hunkered down below it. *If any of them shout for me, my cover will be blown.*

Moments later, the other three crept up and squatted beside him. He let out a breath, relieved that they'd joined him instead of calling after him. Not that he'd ever doubted them.

"Now what?" Julie whispered.

Jake drew his spy camera from his backpack. Winking at her, he tossed it into the air, caught it, and connected it to his smartphone. The screen illuminated, displaying his knee and the slick cobblestone street on its LCD screen. He made a mental note to equip it for night vision when he got home.

"That's great. What's it for? Peeking into the girls' bathroom?" Zach shot Jake a smug leer, and if Jake hadn't known better, he would've sworn he detected a bit of respect. Jake's cheeks flushed. He tried not to pay attention to Maggie, who failed to stifle a giggle.

The window above them was cracked open a few inches. Jake set the camera on the ledge, plugged in the headphones, and positioned the gear on his lap. Zach, Julie, and Maggie leaned in closer.

Part living quarters and part office space, the room housed an ancient kitchenette—with dirty dishes piled high in the sink—a simple oak desk in the center, and, by the door, a junky baker's rack—packed with food containers, dishes, glassware, jars, and knickknacks. The harbormaster reclined on his desk chair, grasping the piece of metal while talking on the phone. He sounded out the Spanish words. "It says, *Cein pasos al sur de ventana de Espana.*"

Jake groaned softly and pressed the heel of his palm into his forehead. *Was he involved with those other men we saw at the church?*

Clearly, the harbormaster wasn't above stealing from

children, and Jake wasn't sure he wanted to discover what other lengths the man might go to for wealth. He returned his attention to the conversation, hoping for new clues.

The man listened for a while. "Right-o. It'll be here," he said, and hung up the phone.

He dropped the piece inside a desk drawer, took a key from his pocket, and locked it. Before leaving the room, he pressed a light switch on the wall, shutting off a nearby floor lamp.

"Now's our chance," Jake whispered. He rose and slid the window open, wincing when it squeaked. He counted to one hundred, and, deciding it was safe, poked his head into the room.

"You're going *inside?*" Maggie and Julie whispered simultaneously.

He withdrew and looked at Zach. "Women," he grumbled.

Zach pushed Jake out of his way. "Move it, twerp. This is finally getting interesting." He climbed through the window. "I got the drawer—you guard the room."

Zach hurdled to the desk, grasped a long letter opener, and went to work picking the lock. Meanwhile, Jake peered down the hall. The shadow of the harbormaster sitting in another room made an ominous silhouette against the open doorway.

Jake gently closed the door, willing it not to creak. Leaving it slightly ajar, he rushed to the corner of the room and unplugged the floor lamp. He then placed the lamp snuggly against the baker's rack and wove the cord around its legs. Using a half-hitch knot, he secured the end of the cord to the doorknob.

"How are you doing?" Jake whispered urgently to Zach.

"Another minute …" Zach kept fiddling with the lock, his face contorting with frustration.

Jake reached into his pocket and rubbed his thumb over his Leatherman. "Zach," he hissed. "Catch!"

Zach seized it, pried open a slender tool, and went to work behind the desk.

Footsteps suddenly reverberated in the hallway.

"Time's up!" Jake vaulted behind the desk next to Zach. "Come on, come on!"

"Got it," Zach said, jamming the tool into the lock with a hard hit. He slid the drawer open and seized the metal piece.

"Hey!" The harbormaster threw the door open. The lamp cord snapped tight, sending the baker's rack and its cargo crashing to the floor.

As he and Zach jumped up, Jake saw the harbormaster stumbling backwards out of the room—unharmed but confused. With the clue safely in hand, they dove out the window and sprinted with the girls down the pier.

Chapter 11

Maggie and Jake arrived home just as Mrs. O'Connell was removing dinner from the oven. "Did you have a good day, Jake?"

He cleared his throat and nodded, hiding a smile. "Yes, ma'am. We went to Skellig Michael."

Mrs. O'Connell spooned a heaping portion of stew onto his plate. "Very nice. I haven't been there since before Maggie was born. To me, it's the marine life that makes Skellig Michael so special. Did you happen to see any puffins or seals?"

Jake and Maggie exchanged wide-eyed glances. "Oh, the tour guide wasn't great, so we missed a lot of stuff," Maggie said.

"That's a shame," Mr. O'Connell said between bites.

Mrs. O'Connell joined them at the table. "So, Jake, is Maggie taking you to the game tomorrow?"

"The game! I almost forgot," Maggie said.

"What game?" Jake asked.

"The first rugby game of the summer. Dingle is playing against our archrivals, Ballyferriter. We haven't beaten them since my brother played."

"Sounds like fun. Can we bring Julie?"

Maggie stabbed her knife into a large piece of potato and waited a moment before answering. Then she let out a breath and smiled at her plate. "Sure. I've got to help Mr. O'Malley round up his sheep for shearing early in the morning. Let's meet at the pub. We can go to the game together from there."

"Want some help with the sheep?" Jake offered.

"Nonsense! No guest of the O'Connells will be laboring on a fine summer's day," Mrs. O'Connell said.

Mr. O'Connell threw his fork onto the table. "Blasted job hunt. My own daughter shouldn't be working her childhood away. A man should be able to provide."

Maggie leaned toward him and grasped his hand. "It's okay, Da. It's only for a bit, until some work comes around. The recession can't last forever."

Jake stared at their entwined fingers. Here was a family that, in hard times, banded together and grew stronger. Families at his school were wealthy beyond belief, yet they tore themselves apart in bitter, petty arguments.

He recalled some of the fights he'd had with his father since the accident, stupid arguments about not buying the latest video game or Blu-ray. But it was never really about getting more stuff. His father's desire to not be a burden, and Jake's attempts to help out, too often collided in their small apartment.

He missed the simple times together, eating pizza and watching the Yankees or working on a science project for school. Sailing. Guilt gnawed at his gut for resenting his father's disability, quickly followed by anguish over being the cause of it. He bit his lip and studied the O'Connells.

His humble, generous host family might be some of the poorest people on the peninsula, but they possessed the most valuable of commodities: family unity.

Better to have family than money.

*   *   *

The next morning, Jake rode his bike to Julie's house to invite her to the rugby match. After the incident with the harbormaster, the group had agreed to take a day off from treasure-hunting. The rugby match served as the perfect distraction. Jake had purposefully left early so as to have plenty of time alone with Julie before the game.

What would he say after inviting her? He hadn't planned that far ahead. *So, after this summer of treasure-hunting, high school should be a breeze, right?* He shook his head and closed his eyes. *Too lame. Weather! Weather always makes for good small talk. The rain here sure is cold.* He groaned. *I am so doomed.*

He cycled up to the house, parked his bike, and ran up to the wraparound porch. He knew his dad would have loved Julie's sponsors' house. It was obviously new, but the architect had done a superb job of making it look like an old-world Irish manor house. After ten minutes of alternating between ringing the doorbell and knocking, he decided to try the back entrance. Maybe Julie's host family was serving brunch in the gazebo. On the way, he peered into the window.

A lightning bolt struck his heart.

Zach and Julie were sitting on a sofa, kissing so passionately that they hadn't heard the doorbell ring. Jake tore himself away from the gut-wrenching scene and kicked at a dirt rock in the yard. It took every ounce of control he had to stop himself from screaming, or crying, or both.

Heartsick, he pedaled toward the pub. When he arrived, he searched for Maggie's bike but didn't see it.

Good. I'll have some time alone.

He trudged into the pub and sat down at the bar, hanging his head and chewing on his lower lip.

The bartender leaned on the counter. "What'll it be, Jake? I'm under strict orders from Mrs. O'Connell to serve you whatever you'd like."

Jake's mouth crimped a little at the sides as he imagined Mrs. O'Connell barking those orders. "I'll have fizzy water with some lime in it, please. Better make it extra lime," he added.

"Oh, *extra* lime. Rough morning, is it?" The bartender set down a napkin and a dish of potato wedges and then slid him his drink.

Jake stirred the limes with a tiny black straw and heaved a sigh. "You could say that."

"I recognize that face. Only a woman can cause such pain," said a strange, raspy voice beside him.

Jake swiveled to see an old man sitting a few stools away. Unshaven and weather-beaten, the man wore an old military jacket with a matching cap and black boots. He offered a bronzed wrinkled hand. "Call me Colonel."

The bartender snickered and rolled his eyes. "Here we go again."

Torn between being polite and being cautious, Jake shook the man's rough but surprisingly strong hand. "Nice to meet you, sir."

The bartender chuckled. "The *Colonel*," he said, sarcasm punching the man's title, "says he's in charge of a special operations unit with the Irish Army. Something top secret, ain't that right, mate?"

The man waved the bartender away.

Jake smiled. "I'm Jake. Jake McGreevy."

"McGreevy?" The Colonel's face lit up. "You got kin around here?"

"My dad had a grandmother in Killorglin."

The old man squinted and lowered his voice. "Wasn't named Noleen, by chance?"

"Yes ... I think she was," Jake said, with considerable surprise.

The Colonel slapped Jake on the knee, his eyes as wide as the sea. "Me lad, she was me mum. That makes me your great-uncle!"

Yeah, right. Jake's dad had warned him that every

Irishman believes he's somehow related to you. Obviously the bartender had been right about this old kook.

"I remember when your da visited us once, when he was a boy. He looked a lot like you, he did, only he had a small scar on his neck, if I recall."

Jake nearly jumped off his stool. "A cat scratched him when he was two!"

"Aye, *that* was it." The Colonel grinned broadly, and Jake smiled back, momentarily dazed. "So, how is he now, lad?"

Jake frowned and dropped his eyes. "He got hurt last year in an accident. He can't walk anymore."

The old man turned Jake's chin and tilted it up, his dark brown eyes locking with Jake's. "He's still your da, isn't he, boy? And you still love him, don't you?"

"Y-yes."

"You hold your head high, then, and talk with pride when you speak of him."

Jake's belly tightened with embarrassment. "Yes, sir."

The man released him. "Now then. Tell me about your girl problems."

Jake sighed, any remaining hesitation giving way to his need for companionship. It wasn't as if he had anybody else to talk to. "Well, there's this girl I like, and I'm pretty sure she liked me, but now she's with somebody else."

"Ah," the Colonel nodded and winked. "And you want to win her back, eh? Just go up and kiss her, man! If it's meant to be, it'll happen."

Jake cringed. "Kiss her? What if she doesn't want me to kiss her?"

The Colonel's guffaw filled the pub. His face turned an unhealthy shade of red, and he clutched his sides as he laughed heartily. Worse, the bartender joined him.

"What?" Jake scowled, humiliated by the second joke

of the day on him. The laughter died down some, and the Colonel wiped a tear from the corner of his eye. "There's a saying, me lad. You can't kiss an Irish girl unexpectedly, just sooner than she thought you would."

Jake shook his head, confused. "She's not Irish. I mean, she has an Irish last name, but she grew up in America."

Both the bartender and the Colonel fell into another bout of laughter, chortling so hard, the glasses hanging over the bar rattled. "Ain't Irish? Then why waste your time?"

Jake smiled, surrendering to their humor.

He spent the rest of the morning at the pub listening intently to the old man's tales about more of his distant relatives. He was lost in another of the Colonel's stories when the pub door opened and Maggie walked in.

"Well, sir, I've got to go." Jake extended his hand to the Colonel.

The old man pulled a card from his pocket. It was blank except for a phone number.

"You ever need anything, anything at all, you call this number, lad. You tell the person on the phone the Colonel's nephew needs help and they'll see to it." The old man tousled Jake's hair and returned to his ale.

Chapter 12

"That man is your *relative?*" Maggie said, pedaling her bike toward the rugby game. "No way."

Jake nodded, struggling to keep up with her as she expertly dodged cars and sped through the busy streets. Growing up in Manhattan hadn't conditioned him to ride a bike as well as Maggie could. "I'm pretty sure. I'll talk to my dad tonight. But he knew stuff he couldn't have known otherwise." Jake was relieved that the conversation had shifted to his great-uncle so quickly after he'd explained that Julie wasn't coming after all.

"Guess you really are tracing your heritage," Maggie said. She steered onto a cement path that led to the stadium. Everyone was pouring into the entrance, each wearing the colors of his or her favorite team. Some had even painted their faces.

Jake dismounted his bike and walked alongside Maggie. "Yep. Should make the report at the end of the summer easy to write."

"Oh, I almost forgot," Maggie said as she handed Jake her brother's rugby jersey.

"What's this for?"

"Well, before you arrived in Dingle, I was thinking you might like to play some rugby while you were here, so my brother called the captain and he put you on the roster," Maggie said.

"I don't understand?" Jake handled the jersey as if it were poisoned.

"Well, if we hadn't got caught up in the treasure hunt, I was going to take you to practice so you could begin playing some games. But to practice, you've got to be on their roster."

Isn't rugby the game where people's limbs fall off? "Oh. Okay, well, I don't know much about rugby, but I like trying new things." Butterflies collided inside Jake's stomach.

"Even if you don't ever want to play," Maggie continued, "wearing the jersey means we can watch from the sidelines with the team. And while we're on the bench, I can tell you what's going on—sort of a play-by-play."

"Well, that sounds okay," Jake said, relief washing over him.

The countdown clock showed twenty minutes to go before the game, yet the sound of the cheering was already building.

Maggie led him to the Dingle bench. She exchanged greetings with several of the team members, hugging them, laughing, and updating them on David's schooling.

Jake hung in the background and shook hands with a few of them. The team was part of a youth league that required players to be under the age of eighteen. He couldn't help but notice that most of them seemed much larger than boys on American high school football teams—larger even than Zach. There was one fellow, though, who was as short as he was, but stockier. "That guy seems a tad out of his league."

Maggie waved to one of the players. "Oh, he's the scrum half. One of his jobs is to wiggle into the pile and steal the ball. See how his ears are taped? That's so they don't get torn."

Jake winced and absently touched one of his own ears. He waited until the players had moved toward the center of the field to start the match before talking with Maggie again. "So what are the rules here?" Jake asked as the action unfolded. "They don't show much rugby in America."

"Well, let's see. Players can run and carry the ball, pass it laterally or backward, or kick it forward. But they can't throw it forward—this isn't like American football. They score by punting it through the uprights, earning three points, or crossing the line and kneeling, which is worth five," Maggie explained. Her excitement about the game—and her in-depth knowledge—made it fun for Jake to learn.

Jake watched in utter amazement as the teams slammed into each other, fighting every moment to move the ball up and down the field and becoming more and more coated with sweat, blood, and grime as the game progressed.

Maggie squinted at the scoreboard and recoiled. "Only five minutes left in the game!" Dingle was down by four points. The referee called a time-out after a few players collided. When one of their players limped toward the bench, Maggie put her hands to her cheeks, moaning, "He was our last substitute. We'll have to forfeit."

Dingle's coaches walked back and forth and scanned their bench. One of them did a double take as his eyes caught Maggie's and then Jake's. He shouted above the rumble of the crowd. "You, there—come here!"

Jake pointed to himself, his eyes opening wide. "Me?"

The coach nodded. "Yeah, you. What's your name?"

"McGreevy. Jake McGreevy." His head was spinning.

"I see," he said scanning his roster. "Here you are. Missed you at practice. I'm Coach Gallagher. Listen, we need you. Ever play rugby before?"

Jake shook his head. "No, Maggie O'Connell's brother signed me up, but—"

"No matter," the coach interrupted. "You don't have to actually *play*, lad. Just stand out there so we can finish the game."

Jake pleaded with Maggie, desperate for her usual voice

of reason. "He can't be serious. I mean, look at me compared to them. I'm—"

"Perfect!" she said. "You have to play, or we'll have to forfeit."

Jake gulped.

"Listen, Jake. You're wearing my brother's jersey—number fourteen. It'll bring you luck!" Maggie found a roll of medical tape and wrapped his ears, tearing the tape with her teeth. Then she winked, her emerald eyes glistening. "Just in case."

With a rush of ... well, something he couldn't begin to describe, Jake trotted onto the field. The fans cheered when the referee restarted the game.

Determined to return home in one piece, Jake kept a safe distance from the others and jogged alongside the action. He was careful to not make eye contact with anybody and did his best to appear busy. From the corner of his eye, he saw the game clock: one minute left.

Suddenly, the ball squirted out of the pile of players and rolled toward him. Time seemed to stop as he looked first at the ball and then at the clock.

The ball appeared to be moving in slow motion.

Forty-five seconds.

Fueled by an unfamiliar drive, he snatched it. Then, gritting his teeth, he charged toward the goal, powered by the cheering of the crowd.

Carrying the odd-shaped ball was awkward, but Jake had one thing going for him: he was *fast*. His eyes steeled, he looked toward the defenders who were positioned between him and the goal line. The one on the left sped straight for Jake like a human bulldozer. Jake spun away from him, barely eluding his grip.

No time to look back.

Jake eyed his remaining rival. The mountain of a boy cast

a wide shadow and seemed to fill the entire goal line. He bared his teeth in a mean grin, as if challenging Jake to even *think* about crossing over.

The crowd counted down the seconds in unison. "Fifteen! Fourteen! Thirteen! ..."

Widening his stance, Jake's opponent raised a filthy hand and waved Jake closer. His legs spread wide, he stamped his feet, priming himself to defend the goal.

"Seven! Six! Five! ..."

Jake remembered his father's motto: *The tougher the obstacle, the more creative you have to be.* He closed the remaining few feet, tucked his chin, and dove between the giant kid's legs, executing a quick somersault and popping to his feet behind the player.

He turned just in time to see the other player, who had been gaining on him again, slam into the defender of the goal line. The two collided, the force of their impact knocking them both to the ground with a crunch.

"Four! Three! Two! ..."

The world went silent as Jake glided across the goal line and knelt to the ground.

"Score!" the referee bellowed, and the shrill screech of his whistle ended the match. Jake stayed in the kneeling position, saying a silent prayer and allowing himself to breathe for the first time in what felt like an eternity.

A crowd descended upon him, and everything blurred as the team carried him around the field in celebration. Maggie ran alongside him, beaming.

*   *   *

"Oh my goodness, whatever happened?" Mrs. O'Connell shrieked when Jake entered the house carrying a prize white rugby ball and sporting a bloodstained rugby jersey.

"We won the game and Jake scored the winning goal,"

Maggie sang as she skipped into the kitchen. She patted Jake on the back, steering him toward her mother, who had been busy skimming through cookbooks for ideas for supper.

Mrs. O'Connell's face blanched as she braced herself against the edge of the counter. After her natural color returned, it darkened to a rich shade of crimson.

"Maggie, you let him play *rugby?* He might have been killed!"

Of all the challengers Jake had faced that day, Mrs. O'Connell was, by far, the most formidable. He took a step backward.

"Oh, you should have *seen* him today," Maggie said, ignoring her mother's concern. "And afterwards, when the players lifted him up—well, his jersey just got a little damaged in the process. But it was fantastic. Oh, and this isn't his blood, mum. There's not a scratch on him—promise!"

Mrs. O'Connell's relief was palpable. Hearing about Jake's triumphs, her face softened and she was able to return to her supper preparations, but only after learning what Jake wanted for dessert.

* * *

His dad was extremely excited when Jake phoned home later that evening to tell him about the Colonel and the rugby match. The conversation lasted longer than most, and when Jake hung up, he felt happier than he had in months.

As he fell into bed and tugged up the covers, he realized today had been the best day he'd had since his dad's accident.

Chapter 13

Jake had to threaten to toss the prize rugby ball into the ocean to get Maggie to agree to let him help with her morning chores. Even though every muscle screamed in protest, he stood beside her at the sheep farm, unpacking and tossing bales of hay into a pen. The wind nipped at their cheeks and whipped some of Maggie's hair free of her ponytail.

She tucked a curl behind her ear. "We should go to the library today. We'll never decipher what Spain's Window is on our own. I did some Internet searches last night after you went to bed and didn't find a thing."

Jake picked up some stray pieces of hay. "Sounds good. I can also search for a genealogy book while we're there. Now that my dad confirmed the Colonel *is* my great-uncle, I think a family tree would be a great graphic for the paper I have to write for school."

"Do you want to call Julie?"

Jake paused. He was still smarting from seeing Julie kissing Zach. It's not as if he didn't think they ever kissed, but catching them in the act had extinguished any remaining glimmers of hope that he might share his first kiss with her. Julie had seemed interested in the treasure hunt, but obviously not enough to unlock lips and answer the door or pick up a phone. "No. Let's pass on Julie and Zach today."

* * *

Jake trotted through the library carrying a huge book and doing his best to balance his pencil and notebook on top. He spotted Maggie taking an old volume about the Spanish Armada down from the shelf.

"Maggie!" he said. Someone shushed him, but he was too excited to care. He dropped the book on the desk and opened it up to a page showing a family tree. "Look at all these McGreevys! And the branch of this tree has my father's grandparents on it."

Maggie joined him at the desk and leaned over the book, standing close enough for him to catch a whiff of her shampoo. "Let's see."

Jake traced the lineage with his finger. "And here's the Colonel. He's the son of my great-grandmother. I'm going to go to the pub later and talk to him some more." He closed the book and turned to face Maggie. "Did you learn anything new?"

"Not yet, but I was about to check out this one." Maggie opened the cover of her book and froze.

Jake leaned in. "What is it?"

"How *could* he?" she seethed, her voice barely above a whisper but full of fury.

Jake followed her gaze. The name *Gerald O'Connell* had been clearly inscribed on the top line of the book's catalogue card.

"Your dad's interested in the Spanish Armada?" Jake said, puzzled.

Maggie slammed the book shut. "No. Oh, NO!"

She ran down the library aisle toward the periodicals section and dug through the stack, grabbing a newspaper from the previous week.

Mystified—as he often was when it came to girls—Jake peered over her shoulder. "Mid-Week Bandits? What do they have to do with your father?"

Maggie grimaced, reading a portion of the article. "'The Mid-Week Bandits have struck on *Tuesdays and Thursdays*, targeting Spanish artifacts.'"

Jake blinked. "Oh. Tuesdays and Thursdays are the days your dad's gone, right?"

Maggie nodded, her cheeks a vibrant shade of red. "Yeah. And he's been so secretive, using the back room of the house. He locks it and takes the key, and he keeps dropping phrases like, 'I hope all this pays off.'"

Jake put a hand on her shoulder and gave her a comforting squeeze. "I'm sure it's a coincidence. He couldn't be involved with anything like that." He hoped the doubt in his voice wasn't too apparent.

"He'd jolly well better not be! But until we know for sure, the treasure hunt will have to wait." Maggie's eye twitched and her face hardened with stress.

Jake worked his mouth into a forced smile. "That's okay. My brain needs a rest from the riddle of Spain's Window, anyway."

I need to find that treasure, but Maggie needs help.

Chapter 14

Jake's thighs burned from squatting for over an hour behind the hedgerow outside the O'Connells' house. He observed Maggie, who was sitting next to him stoically and showing no sign of discomfort.

"There he goes!" she whispered. The family car motored past, and Jake and Maggie mounted their bikes and pedaled after it. Thankfully, the tourist traffic leading into town kept Mr. O'Connell from driving at his normal pace. Still, Jake panted as he pumped his legs on the rusty pedals.

He couldn't believe that he was tailing his host. Of all the daring things he'd done recently, following an adult whom he suspected of being a crook was a new experience. "Won't your dad see us in the rearview mirror?"

"No," Maggie called back, "it fell off a year ago!"

They followed the vehicle through the crowded streets of Dingle until the old cobblestone roads gave way to smooth pavement. Free of the tourist traffic now, Mr. O'Connell stepped on the gas.

"Faster!" Maggie stood up as she rode, trying to exert every ounce of strength and speed, but the distance between them and Mr. O'Connell expanded. She cursed and slammed on her brakes.

Jake whizzed past her before locking up his own wheels and skidding to a halt. "What?"

She leaned over her handlebars, breathing hard and

pointing straight ahead. "That's Conor Pass, one of the highest roads in all of Ireland. We'll never make it up."

The road ahead of them wound its way up the mountain with several switchbacks, and the sound of Mr. O'Connell's car coughing up the hill faded in the distance.

Jake looked back at Maggie. "Know anybody who can drive us around?"

"No, I'm afraid not. I'll be getting my learner's permit next year so that I can drive for my job on the farm. But that doesn't help us now."

"Probably not," Jake nodded.

"On the other hand, my brother *did* teach me how to drive before he left," Maggie said. "And ..."

"And *what?*" Jake asked. "Tell me."

"And he was a really good teacher ..." Maggie sat up straight and gave Jake a sly smile. "I have an idea."

* * *

Jake kept guard while Maggie forced her weight against the barn door. It creaked open, and Jake ducked, covering himself with his arms as dozens of swallows fluttered out.

"Come on. It's over here." Maggie walked into the barn and crossed to a large tarp-covered object. "Give me a hand with these, would you?"

They moved several old chicken cages and assorted farm tools off the top. Dust erupted from the canvas as Maggie drew it back to reveal an old car.

Her face beamed with the pride of a new Ferrari owner. "What do you think?"

Jake scratched his head. "I'm glad my tetanus shots are up to date."

She put her hands on her hips. "It's a classic—a 1962 Vauxhall Cresta. Even Queen Elizabeth drove one. My brother found it in a barn near Dublin and has been restoring it ever since."

"Restoring? I'd hate to see the way he found it."

Maggie grumbled and wiped a bit of dust from the fender. "Well, sure, he hasn't gotten too far, but he did have her running once."

Once was good enough. "Okay, let's get to work."

Jake removed his jacket and approached the antique in the same way he would one of the broken rejects he'd inherited at the security shop: instead of bemoaning its current state of ruin, he focused on its potential. Helping Maggie clean the Cresta, he felt the first spark of optimism. It wasn't in such bad shape after all.

Methodically, he checked the hoses and the wires under the hood for obvious problems and made a list of necessary repairs. The patch-up ate into the rest of Tuesday and all of Wednesday, but an hour before dinner, the car was officially roadworthy.

Jake opened the driver's door for Maggie and bowed. "Your carriage, m'lady."

She giggled and slid into the driver's seat. Seconds later, her mood soured. "Problem."

"What?" Jake leaned into the car. She pointed at the ignition. The key lock cylinder was dangling from the steering column, exposing a tangle of wires behind. Jake pursed his lips. "Hmm."

Maggie moved to the passenger seat to allow Jake a better view. He fingered the exposed wires. "Looks like it's been hotwired."

"What are you waiting for, then?"

"Excuse me?"

"Come on, Mr. New York City Gadget Geek. Surely you can hotwire a car." She crossed her arms and looked at him expectantly, her lips curling into a playful smile.

Jake tried to recall the steps he'd have to take. He did

know one thing: he couldn't let her down. He bit the inside of his cheek and struggled to make sense of the mess of wires and parts.

"Okay. These loose red and white wires are supposed to be attached to the back of the key tumbler." Showing the wires to Maggie, he said, "You touch them together and …"

The engine suddenly cranked, making the seats rumble, but it didn't catch.

Maggie's eyes shone bright in the dim light of the car. "Wow, I didn't realize it was that easy."

Jake shrugged. Although what he really wanted to do was celebrate his luck. *Neither did I.*

"Well, the newer cars are a lot harder, but these old ones don't have much security. My father had an old truck at our summer place that had no key, so that's how we'd start it." He stuffed the wires inside their proper locations and slid the tumbler back into the steering column. "Now we need something to hold it in place. Got any glue or tape?"

Maggie scanned the barn. "I don't see any. Don't you Americans always have gum?"

"Good idea." Jake rooted through his backpack and found a stick of gum. He chewed it rapidly and then used it to form a thin ring around the switch. "That'll work." He jumped out and let Maggie slide back behind the wheel.

She gently turned the key, and once again the engine cranked but didn't start. "Sounds like the battery is still good. I wonder why it won't go?"

Jake thought for a moment. "Whenever my dad and I took the boat out from winter storage, we'd have to pour a little gas into the carburetor before the trolling motor would work." He scanned the barn with his eyes and spotted a gas can next to a rototiller. He found a small glass jar on the workbench and poured some of the fuel into it. "When I say go, turn the key." He climbed onto the bumper, opened the hood, and balanced himself above the engine. Removing the air filter, he prepared to dump gas into the carburetor. "Go!"

The engine started to turn over, sputtering and coughing.

Maggie pumped the gas pedal and Jake watched the butterfly valve on the carburetor open. Slowly, he poured some fuel into the iron monster's hungry throat. Suddenly, the engine caught and sent up a flash of smoke, knocking Jake off the car.

"Oh my gosh!" Maggie ran over to him, concern written all over her dirt-smeared face. Jake sat up, dazed. The stench of burning hair seared his nostrils and he wiped a thick coat of soot from his face with one finger.

Then he started laughing—so hard that tears fell from his eyes and his belly ached. Maggie joined in, and they sat on the ground together, bursting with happiness, the car's engine purring gently beside them.

Chapter 15

Thursday afternoon, Maggie and Jake were perched on the hood of the Cresta at the top of Conor Pass, waiting for Mr. O'Connell to drive by. A leafy tree hid them from the road.

"So …" Jake stopped himself.

"What?"

She already worries her dad's a crook. I can't press her any further. "Nothing."

"Come on, Jake. We're friends. What is it?" Maggie urged.

He took a deep breath. "Well, I'm just wondering … if your dad is out of work, why did your family agree to sponsor a student for the summer?"

She gazed at the ocean far below. "My parents want me to have every possible experience and advantage. They had this idea that if I made some friends from the United States, later I might be able to visit or even move there."

Sounds like her parents—always taking care of her. "I'd love to help, but I don't think America has anything to offer that you don't already have here," he said.

"My da has this romantic impression of life in the U.S. from watching reruns of *Happy Days* and *The Brady Bunch*."

Jake laughed. "Those shows are total stereotypes. It would be like my thinking every Irish girl has red hair and does step dancing. Oh, wait …"

She gave him a little shove, but he was happy to see that she cracked a smile.

Jake leapt from the car's hood. "Check this out." He fished

in his pocket for his yo-yo and performed a few tricks with it. Maggie's eyes lit up.

"I haven't seen one of those in years!"

"I'm kind of too old for it, but it was my dad's from his childhood. It goes everywhere with me."

"Can I try it?"

"Go for it." Jake handed Maggie the wooden toy, and she stuck her finger through the small wire loop. "This isn't string."

"Yeah, the string broke, so I fixed it with 200-pound fishing line from my tackle box. Much stronger, and it doesn't fray."

Maggie flicked her wrist and the yo-yo spun down and right back up, hitting her palm with a slap. "Nice."

The telltale sputtering of the O'Connell family car interrupted them. They jumped into the Cresta and Maggie started the engine. A few moments later, Mr. O'Connell whizzed by.

"Hit it!" Jake shouted.

Maggie floored the accelerator. The old beater wouldn't win any shows, but the engine was strong and the rear tires spit up gravel as it jumped back out onto the road.

They followed Mr. O'Connell over the hill and into the town of Cloghane, where he parked at the curb of a shop-filled street.

"Guess we're on foot now," Jake said.

Maggie pulled over and parked a block and a half behind her dad's car. They kept close to the storefronts, ducking into alleyways or behind postal boxes. At the end of the block, Mr. O'Connell stopped on a street corner. A few moments later, a van pulled up to him. He stepped up to the window and shook the driver's hand.

Maggie gasped when she saw the man's face. "It's the guy from the church!"

Jake squinted. "You don't know that for sure. We didn't see him. Only Julie did."

"But didn't she say he had a pointy nose and wire-rimmed glasses?"

Jake didn't respond, mesmerized by watching Mr. O'Connell walk to the other side of the van and climb in. The stranger shifted the vehicle into gear and sped away.

Maggie twisted her hair and pulled on it, emitting an anguished squeal. "They're going to do another heist! Come on—we've got to stop them!" She started running back up the street.

Boy, she's fast. Jake pumped his legs and caught up to her as she neared the Cresta. "Stop!" He grabbed her arm and spun her around.

"What are you doing?" she cried.

"They're gone. We can't catch them. Besides, there could be a million reasons for what we just saw."

Maggie spoke through clenched teeth. "Name one."

Jake stared at the van as it disappeared from sight, searching for something—anything—to reassure her. He had zilch.

"Well, well. If it isn't Dingle's new rugby hero," a scratchy voice called from behind.

Jake pivoted and found himself nose-to-nose with an enormous ebony horse. He stumbled backward, bumping into Maggie.

"That was the most brilliant ending to a game I've seen in a dog's age. No doubt they'll be talking about it for years and years."

Jake's eyes darted up from the horse's face and saw that the creature was attached to a buggy, and the voice was coming from its driver. The man was about his father's age, dressed in a tuxedo and top hat, which did little to make his rough skin and unshaven jaw appear less scruffy. Permanent laugh lines bracketed his eyes and mouth.

"Th-thank you, sir," Jake stammered.

"No need for formality, lad. O'Brien's the name. Nolan O'Brien," he said, tipping his hat. "How about a ride round the village? Free of charge for the man who crushed those Balleyferriter punks."

Jake looked at the animal and then at Maggie, his palms growing slick with sweat. He moved backwards, searching desperately for a good excuse.

"Oh, let's do it!" Maggie said. "Might help take our mind off my da."

Jake shook his head vigorously. "I'm—I'm not into horses."

"Huh? What do you mean? It's just a carriage ride."

"My dad … his accident … it was on a horse," Jake stammered. "This is the closest I've been to one since …"

"Oh. I'm so sorry." Maggie was crestfallen.

"Ah, don't go fretting about this horse now, sonny. This one here is so worn out, the glue folks turned her away. She won't bother ye," the driver called out.

Maggie gazed at the carriage longingly. Jake could tell that she really wanted to go. Carriage rides weren't something her family could afford to do.

Nothing that happened in my past is her fault. And the horse does seem kind of tired. Plus, it's hooked to the carriage.

"Let's go." Jake offered his hand to Maggie and helped her into the seat, staying well clear of the horse.

As they clopped through the village streets, the driver jabbered on about the different sites of interest, speaking animatedly and with the air of a Broadway actor until they emerged on the other side of the town. He slowed when the road began to incline. "Gotta turn around now. My poor old mare doesn't like to climb hills anymore."

"Hill? That's a mountain," Jake said.

The driver cracked the reins. "Indeed, it is. That's Mount Brandon. Name stems from our legendary navigator, St. Brendan. They say, if you're at the top on a clear day, you can see all the way to Spain."

Jake and Maggie turned to each other and spoke as one. "Spain's Window!"

Chapter 16

The carriage driver dropped them off a few blocks from the car. Shadowy clouds were filling the sky, and a low rumble suggested that a storm was imminent.

"We'd better run for it," Maggie said.

Thunder banged overhead and the clouds suddenly released their load, drenching the streets. By the time Maggie and Jake arrived at the car, water dripped from them both, making their hair and clothes cling to their skin.

Jake's chattering teeth made speaking nearly impossible. "St-start the car and let's hope the h-heat works."

Maggie started the ignition, and the engine rattled to life. She exhaled a relieved sigh and stepped on the accelerator, revving the engine.

Jake jammed his fingers against the heating vent. "Feels like it's working. Rev the gas again."

As she did so, Maggie slicked her hair into a makeshift ponytail. Her face glistened in the afternoon light, and Jake stared at her, unable to break away from the aura surrounding her. She turned to him and he blushed, something he seemed to do a lot around her.

She smiled sweetly and an unseen force pushed them toward each other. Jake's body surged with electricity as her face drew closer to his. He closed his eyes, readying himself for what would happen next.

My first kiss …

But the moment their lips touched, an icy river of water crashed over them.

Maggie shrieked as they jumped apart, and Jake glared at the car's sagging, darkened fabric lining the car's roof.

"I guess my brother didn't get around to fixing this," Maggie grumbled. Jake pressed a hand against the soaked felt, making more water pour into the car. "We'd better go."

So much for kissing.

During the ride home, Jake tried to focus on the scenery. He tensed every muscle in his body in an effort to keep from shaking, both from being cold and from what had just happened. The topics of conversation stayed well away from Maggie's dad or the interrupted kiss.

As the car crested Conor Pass, the sky parted, revealing a sparkling ocean bathed in sunlight below. Maggie pulled the car over at a lookout point beside the road.

"I never grow tired of this," she sighed, gazing dreamily at the water. "It's magical every time you look at it."

"You should see the Caribbean. There are so many different shades of blue, it's like a painting." Jake felt a lump in his throat and wished away the tears that were threatening to form.

Maggie reached over and squeezed his hand. Her skin warmed his. "Is the ocean your bond with your da?"

The strength in her hand flowed through him as he laced his fingers with hers. "We were really close. Before he was paralyzed, we'd sail every summer and even take a month off from school during the winter. He has disability insurance, but we had to sell the sailboat to pay the medical bills. We also moved from our house into an apartment building for handicapped people."

"*Were* close? He's still your father."

Jake tried to soften the edge in his voice. "It's different now."

Maggie nodded thoughtfully. "Think you'll ever go back to the Caribbean?"

"One day." Jake focused on the ocean, fighting the renewed surge of emotion. "There's this island, uncharted and relatively unknown. It has a waterfall, a freshwater pool, and tons of natural fruits. My dad says that that's where he proposed to my mom."

"Sounds beautiful."

He looked down. "It's also where he placed her ashes when she died."

"Oh, Jake," she said, her voice quiet, and no less full of emotion than his.

"If I get enough money, I'll buy back the schooner and convert it into a single-hander, something I can manage myself. Then I'll take my dad there and it'll be like old times." He looked into Maggie's eyes then and realized that she, too, was near tears.

Squeezing his hand, she rested her forehead against his. "Maybe the treasure will be your ticket."

Jake nodded.

Not maybe. I'm going to get that treasure.

*   *   *

Maggie unlocked the door and led the way into the kitchen. She picked up a note on the counter and wrinkled her nose.

"What's it say?" Jake asked.

"My aunt in Killarny is sick. My mum's gone there overnight and says my da is going to meet her there to take care of my cousins until my aunt comes home from the hospital."

"That's too bad." Jake was secretly glad her parents weren't home. Maggie needed to wait to confront her father until they had further evidence. "Guess we'll spend tomorrow searching for the next clue."

"Sounds good," she said as she opened the refrigerator. Relief showed on her face—she wasn't ready to challenge her father either. "Should we call Zach and Julie?"

Jake grabbed a dinner roll from the table, taking his time to chew. Attempting to appear uninterested, he said, "I guess."

Julie told them Zach had food poisoning and she wanted to stay with him. Jake snickered at the image of Zach puking his guts out, but then, when he thought of Julie with him, he suddenly realized it didn't bother him.

That's a first.

Chapter 17

Jake yawned and trudged upward, still tired from having helped Maggie with her early-morning chores.

She hiked up the rocky path, keeping a few steps ahead of him, with an ease that made Jake vow to beef up his workout routine when he returned home.

He tried to focus on the terrain as opposed to Maggie's legs. She was wearing knee-high socks with a plaid skirt, and watching it swish back and forth was making him blush—and the strenuous hike more enjoyable.

"Your backpack looks fuller today," she called back to him. "What'd you pack?"

"Rain poncho. Learned my lesson."

"A good Irishman loves the rain—has to, since he sees it practically every day!" Maggie grinned, slowing to admire a patch of yellow flowers.

Jake thought for a moment about the rainy days in New York. He had always liked to go outside and walk in the rain when everyone else was running for cover. *Maybe I am Irish.* He stopped next to Maggie and checked the map, using the break to catch his breath. "We're almost there. Whatever the window is, it should be around here somewhere."

"Well, come on then. Let's go."

An hour later, they crested the final summit. The soreness from the hike vanished as Jake drank in the view below—an emerald patchwork quilt of farms, creeks, and flagstone cairns on one side and miles of blue ocean on the other.

Maggie twirled around. "Wow, you *can* see a long way from up here."

"Look!" Jake pointed to a rock formation behind her. Dozens of gigantic boulders had toppled from the peak of the hill. One had landed atop two others, forming a natural stone window frame.

Maggie squealed and raced toward it, with Jake following closely behind and scanning for clues. An unexpected shower took them by surprise, but their excitement trumped any worry.

Maggie stood next to the formation and peered in every direction. "Fifty steps," she said. "But which way?"

"Toward Spain, I'd guess." He took out his compass to orient himself.

A deep voice came up from behind them, and Jake froze.

"What was that?" Maggie whispered.

"Shhh." Jake grabbed her and led her behind the boulders. They crouched, listening for more.

"The boss'd better be right. I'm fed up walkin' through the middle of nowhere," said a familiar gruff voice.

Jake squinted through the gaps between the rocks. "There're two of them," he whispered to Maggie. "I think they're the ones from the church. But the big one is definitely that guy Malic, who tried to mug Julie and me."

Maggie's eyes widened with fear. "Were they following us?"

Jake shrugged and watched as the men turned in their direction.

"Can you see the other one? Is he the one who met my da?" Maggie asked.

"I can't tell from here."

"I have to know!" She tried to crawl to a better spot, but Jake reached for her.

"No, Maggie, stop!"

She inched closer. Resting her knee on a pile of stones, she lost her balance when she leaned too far forward. The small stones scattered beneath her, and the hard crunching sound seemed to ricochet across the peninsula.

"Whassat?" Malic said.

"There, behind the boulders!" the other one called, heading toward Jake.

"Run!" Jake yelled, pulling Maggie up.

She resisted at first. "I want to find out what's going on with my da!"

"No, Maggie, we're outgunned. Let's go!" Jake pulled her toward the path downhill.

"Faster—they're going to catch us!"

With Maggie in his grip, Jake veered off the path. He was running at breakneck speed when his eyes caught a glimpse of wide-open sky all around him. He skidded to a halt. Dirt from his feet sprayed from the towering cliff into the abyss below. He tackled Maggie to keep her from plunging off the mountain.

"We're trapped!" she screamed.

"There!" Jake pointed out a section of cliff that wasn't a vertical drop, but a steep rocky slope. The rainwater was washing down the cliff face, forming a natural water slide. "We'll use the poncho."

He tore it from his backpack.

"No way—we could die!" she said.

But the sound of the men approaching won out. Maggie and Jake strode quickly toward the stream of water. He unfolded the poncho and they both sat down on it, Jake in front, with Maggie's arms wrapped around his waist.

Malic broke free of the brush. "Stop, you brats!"

"Go!" Jake yelled. He and Maggie clawed at the ground to start their makeshift bobsled down the hill.

The giant reached for Maggie but she chucked a stone at him. He fell to the ground, grasping his face.

The slow takeoff morphed into a rapid descent down the rock chute. Maggie screamed and wrapped her arms tighter around Jake. He held the corners of the poncho up and leaned into the curves while they raced through the sluiceway. They ducked, whizzing by a low tree limb overhead. Jake's heart lurched as he saw the rockslide slope upward, forming a jump.

"Hang on!"

Plummeting with the force of a roller coaster, they hit the ramp and were launched into the air. Time paused while they were airborne and then rudely fast-forwarded as they slammed into a deep puddle.

Spitting out mouthfuls of mud, Jake stood up, grateful that the muck came only to his thighs. Maggie sat in the puddle, her head bent and her body shaking so hard he worried she might fall apart. He ran to her and clutched her arm. "Are you all right?"

She raised her chin and brushed her hair away, smearing dirt across her forehead and cheeks. She was crying, but from laughter. "What a *rush!*"

Jake began laughing too. "Did you get a look at the skinny guy?"

"No, it happened too fast."

He dug through his backpack. "Can't find the map."

"All it would tell us is that we're on the wrong side of the mountain from our car. So which way do you want to walk?" Maggie said, rising to her feet.

"Doesn't much matter to me. I'm just happy to be alive!" he said.

Chapter 18

Without a defined trail, it took hours for Jake and Maggie to carefully descend the rest of the way down the steep rocky slope. They reached the bottom at the same moment the final rays of sunlight dissolved on the horizon, draining every trace of color from the sky. A quick glance at his watch showed the time to be 9:45 PM. Looking back at the incredible terrain they'd traversed, Jake suppressed a shiver. "Good thing Irish days are so long. We never would've found our way off the mountain in the pitch black."

"Don't celebrate yet," Maggie said, with an edge in her voice. "Finding a path could take hours, not to mention getting back home. And my mother ..." Her eyes widened and she swallowed hard. "It will not be good."

Jake's heart crash-landed in his stomach. With all the enthusiasm of a funeral march, he and Maggie held hands and navigated their way across the mountain's base. The unfamiliar noises of the night startled them, every new snap or caw making them flinch and step closer until their shoulders pressed together.

Jake cleared his throat and put his effort into ignoring the night terrors. "What I don't understand is how those goons knew to hike up Mount Brandon."

Maggie squeezed Jake's hand so tightly that he feared she'd turn it to diamonds. "It just proves it. My father's a crook." She spun to face him now, her voice cracking with anxiety. "I told my mum we were going to hike Mount Brandon. I bet she told my da."

Jake touched her cheek, his heart thudding heavily. "You have to have faith in your father."

She sniffed, dismissing him. Then she stopped and pointed to a glow on the horizon. "Do you see that?"

"Yeah, I wonder what it is."

"Hopefully, it's not those thugs." They crept toward the strange light, shuffling their feet to avoid breaking branches or making other noises that might attract attention. The outlines of trucks and trailers and people surrounding a towering bonfire materialized before them. The smell of animals and fresh hay wafted on the night breeze.

"*Whisht*, be still—tinkers," Maggie whispered, grabbing Jake's sleeve and pulling him back.

"Translate?"

She held out her arm, barring him from moving forward. "Well, they're called travelers now. They're like gypsies. They live in their trailers and sell stuff on the side of the road. Clusters of families have been doing it for generations. Most are harmless, but you never know."

The landscape had lost its distinct features and they could no longer see more than ten feet ahead. Without the moon as their guide, they would have easily become lost. Jake sighed, realizing their options had vanished with the sunlight. "We're still wet and the temperature is dropping. Neither of us has more than a light jacket, and we have no food or water."

Maggie eyed the travelers, then her outfit, and finally Jake. A deflated sigh escaped her lips. "Okay, but we're going in together. Be careful."

He grinned. "When have I not been careful?"

She bumped him playfully. "Let's see, in the last week I've watched you nearly drown in Blasket Sound, break into the harbormaster's office, and fall off an exploding car. Not to mention that today, we slid down the side of a mountain on your *poncho*. Call me crazy. Still, I'm exercising a few precautions."

"Gee, when you put it that way, I guess it's a good thing I keep you around." Jake bent his arm and offered it to Maggie. Smirking, she hooked her arm through his.

As they got closer, the aroma of cooking meat enveloped them, making Jake suddenly aware of how hungry he was. Laughter, conversation, and the chatter of children playing became audible, and a few minutes later, faces became clear. Most of the trailers weren't for camping, as Jake had expected, but were instead for livestock. Jake could see several large draft horses and ponies of different varieties tied up alongside. *Just my luck.*

They had come upon what appeared to be a group of families gathered at a campground. Some played instruments—a combination of strings, drums, and harmonicas, even homemade ones—reminding Jake of the street bands by Central Park. Nothing ominous tripped his internal alarms.

Stopping at the edge of the camp, Maggie called out, "Good evening! Mind if we enter your camp?"

As if the power off button had been hit on a radio, the cacophony ceased. Everybody paused, their attention fixated on Jake and Maggie. Jake's heart thundered and his palms began to sweat.

Please let them be friendly.

A lean middle-aged man with long rusty-colored hair stood and approached them. "Who'd be wanting to join us?"

Maggie cleared her throat, her body trembling against Jake's as she crowded closer to him. "Two souls weary from a day of travel."

Jake raised an eyebrow. *Women are so dramatic.*

Maggie leaned in and whispered, "I read somewhere that tinkers use that greeting."

A murmuring broke the silence, and somebody said, "Ah, they're just kids."

"By all means, join us," the man called. He clapped his hands twice, the thwacks booming like gunshots. "Come."

Jake and Maggie ambled toward the leader, their legs moving as if through tar.

"Name's Patrick O'Hara." The man seized Jake's hand, shaking it with gusto. "You two look like a couple of drowned rats. Darcie, please bring some food for our guests."

A tall, plainly dressed woman nodded and climbed into a trailer only to return moments later with a plate of biscuits. She smiled as she offered it to them, revealing her crooked graying teeth. Jake and Maggie each took one, their mouths watering.

"This is the best thing I've ever eaten." Jake closed his eyes, relishing the warm, fatty bread. He tried to catch the crumbs dribbling down his chin, and not wanting to waste another morsel, he stuffed the rest of the biscuit into his mouth.

Maggie pierced him with a powerful stare, her eyes glinting impishly. "You said the same thing about my mother's shepherd's pie."

Laughter ensued, and the tension in the camp dissipated. The music started back up and conversations resumed.

Patrick offered more biscuits. "What brings you to our lovely camp?"

Jake removed one from the plate, handed it to Maggie, and took another for himself. "We were hiking on Mount Brandon and got lost."

Patrick's head fell back and he laughed so heartily his chest shook. "Are you telling me you got lost on the mountain named for a navigator?"

Jake nodded and smiled at the irony.

Patrick sipped from a canteen and wiped his lips with the cuff of his sleeve. "We can take you to the trailhead tomorrow."

"Not on horseback ...?" Jake's heart started pounding.

"Nah. Those horses are for working the farmer's fields and such. Most haven't been ridden in years. We'll take you in one of the vans in the morning. 'Fraid tonight you're stuck with us." Patrick smiled.

Jake swallowed the last bite of biscuit, licked his fingers, and warmed his hands by the fire. "A warm fire, music, and biscuits. Not a bad life."

An uncomfortable silence thickened the air. Patrick stared at the flickering fire. "This life may seem romantic, lad, but it ain't. See that girl there?" He gestured toward a young girl sleeping with her head on a woman's lap. "That's my daughter. Living like this, she'll get no education, no skills. She'll have no choice but to grow up a traveler."

Embarrassment flushed Jake's cheeks even more than the fire had. Choosing his words more carefully, he said, "Couldn't you settle somewhere and find a job?"

"What's the wage for storytelling, lad? That's my only skill." Patrick hurled a couple of logs on the fire. Stirring the ashes with a metal staff, he stoked the flames at least six feet high, sending crackling embers into the night.

Maggie nudged Jake and nodded toward their host as he stabbed the earth with the blazing poker. Jake followed Maggie's gaze and observed that the poker was oddly shaped and, illuminated by the fire, it seemed to have some sort of engraving on it. "Excuse me, sir ... May I see that?"

Patrick shrugged and handed it to him, more interested in the contents of his canteen than the rusty piece of metal.

Jake feigned nonchalance as he rubbed his fingers over the notches in the staff. They appeared to be a perfect fit for the other puzzle pieces. He flipped the staff over and bit his tongue. Spanish writing was engraved on the other side.

No way.

"Where did you get this?" Maggie asked, gripping Jake's sleeve.

Patrick raised his canteen to his lips and crooked one leg over the other. "Not far from here. On top of your Mount Brandon, actually, sticking up from the ground. Must have been ten years ago."

Jake handed it back to him. He had done his fair share of negotiating with street vendors, and he understood that the moment he showed more than slight interest in something, the price would rise. He took a slow deep breath and steadied his nerves. "It's kind of cool. Can I buy it from you? As a souvenir?"

Patrick's eyes narrowed. He angled his head and smiled, a dimple pitting his cheek. "This boy wants to buy me fire poker," he announced to the camp.

The laughter that followed was far from polite. Of course, how many American boys wandered their way into camps and asked to buy seemingly useless found objects when the travelers sold handcrafted wares?

Great. I've blown it.

Patrick clamped a solid warm palm on Jake's shoulder. "You don't just buy something like this. An object of unknown value is best wagered for."

The weight of the camp's eyes pressed on Jake more heavily than Patrick's hand. Maggie stared at the violin resting beside Patrick with an expression Jake was rapidly learning meant trouble.

Before he could stop her, she stood and pointed at the instrument. "How about a competition?" She tipped her head toward Jake. "He's a fiddler back in the U.S."

Patrick's eyes glinted in the light of the fire. "Ah, but if we're playing the fiddle, we must have dancing!"

Now it was Maggie's turn to panic. Her expression changed from one of calculation to one of dread.

Patrick clapped his hands together. "Let's pair up. Me and my Darcie versus the two of ye."

"I ... I don't—" Maggie's eyes darted to Jake as if he would come to her rescue. He knew this would be the last time Maggie would volunteer him for something without asking. Grinning sideways at her, he offered his hand to Patrick. "It's a bet."

Maggie's scowl seared his cheeks.

"What are you wagering?" Patrick asked.

Jake pulled his smartphone from his backpack. "This. The phone part doesn't work here, since I don't have the international plan, but you can still play games and take pictures and stuff."

Patrick pressed buttons and tested the screen until he appeared satisfied. He returned it to Jake and picked up his violin. "Let's play then."

Someone handed Jake a violin and a bow. As he plucked the strings and twisted the screws to tune it, the crowd moved back from the fire. Five men carried in slabs of wood to form a makeshift dance floor. Jake stole a glance at Maggie, who was glaring at him while warming up her muscles.

Darcie stretched her calves and Patrick plucked his violin strings, neither showing any sign of nerves. Then the traveler raised his cheek to his wife, and she gave him a peck before strutting onto the dance floor.

Patrick struck up a lively tune that Jake didn't recognize but soon found himself tapping his foot to. Darcie danced in perfect time with her husband, the patter of her shoes tapping throughout the camp.

Jake and Maggie shared a nervous glance. The travelers clapped and hollered, raising their drinks and stomping their feet as Darcie and Patrick finished and bowed.

His confidence in Maggie unwavering, Jake whispered one word to her: "Riverdance."

Maggie gave him a brief trembling smile and took her place. Jake stood, held his chin high, and raised his bow, waiting for Maggie's signal.

After a moment that stretched to eternity, she nodded.

Jake tried to ignore the murmur pulsing through the crowd as he began to play—mostly surprise and praise for his talent. From the corner of his eye, he watched Maggie, who danced with restrained energy, missing a few steps. Frustration played on her face.

Uh-oh.

At the end of the song, Jake joined her and they bowed. Maggie closed her eyes and breathed heavily, her whole body shaking. The crowd rewarded them with a polite golf clap and a few mumbles of approval.

Patrick inclined his head to Jake and grinned with obvious confidence. "Not bad, not bad. Let's have it all out then, eh, my love?" He attacked the strings with his bow. The crowd clapped in rhythm, and Darcie's feet blurred on the floor.

Maggie turned to Jake. "I'm sorry—it's been too long. I can't dance the way I used to."

He clasped her hands and his eyes met hers. "Since the day I met you, I haven't seen you back down from anything. Just let the music flow through you. Don't worry about the stakes. Dance because you love dancing."

Maggie closed her eyes and rested her forehead against his. He was about to hug her when the crowd applauded, signaling the end of Patrick and Darcie's performance.

Maggie broke away and moved to the center of their

impromptu dance floor. She crossed one leg in front of the other and cocked her ankle. She stared at her feet, her breath visible in the cool night air. The only sound was an occasional snap from the fire.

This time she didn't appear scared or unsure of herself. She didn't fidget or tremble or bite her lip. She commanded the attention of everybody who watched, as if silently daring anyone to so much as think about doubting her.

They don't stand a chance.

Jake raised his bow and waited for her cue. A strange calm overtook him, along with the sudden knowledge that something extraordinary was about to happen. Quickly, he switched his smartphone to video-record mode and propped it against a log, hopeful it was in focus.

Maggie opened her eyes and raised her head. She stared at Jake for a few seconds and winked.

The sharp note of Jake's first stroke split the late-evening silence. He closed his eyes and let the increasing rhythm of Maggie's steps guide his fingers across the strings, the familiar notes rushing back to him. Arms pinned at her sides and torso erect, Maggie danced as never before—her legs flashing with each step, her feet striking the floor with ferocity and speed.

As his fingers plucked the strings ever faster, Jake scanned the crowd. They weren't clapping or cheering as they'd done with Darcie, but they were watching in wonderment as the young girl gave her soul to the dance. She spun around and around, Jake's playing matching her every step. Her skirt flew out from the force of her twirl. The centrifugal force spun any remaining dampness from her clothing, the resulting mist mixing with the fire and creating an angelic aura around her.

Jake hit the last note and pressed firmly on the strings, concluding with a dramatic finish. Maggie slid into a split and dropped her head in a final bow.

A hush overcame the camp for a moment, the calm before the thunderous storm of applause. Maggie jumped up and ran to Jake, pulling him into a vice-like hug.

Tears sparkled in her eyes. Tears of joy, tears of release at having remembered how much she did indeed love to dance.

Patrick made his way through the crowd. "Well, if that wasn't the dandiest thing I ever saw." He hugged Maggie and winked at Jake. "And you play a pretty good fiddle too, me lad."

Jake nodded and exhaled for the first time in several minutes.

"I believe this is now yours."

The crowd cheered again as Patrick handed Jake the carved poker, and despite the late hour, another round of ale was opened to celebrate the exceptional performance they had just witnessed.

Chapter 19

Jake pushed the remnants of his stew away and stared at their prize. Nervous energy was causing his leg to twitch. They were close to finding the treasure. He could feel it. When the whirlwind night of singing and dancing ended, Jake hadn't wanted to leave his new traveler friends. He and Maggie had spent the remainder of the night under the stars, lying by the glowing embers of the fire on blankets loaned to them by the tinkers.

Mrs. O'Connell met them at the door the next morning and scolded them soundly for being out all night. Then she whipped up a hot breakfast and lectured them some more.

Maggie sat next to Jake, her ears crimson from the tongue-lashing. "Did you translate the writing yet?" she whispered.

"No, I wanted to wait for you." He pulled the smartphone from his backpack.

Maggie leaned in to read the small screen. Her hair, still damp from her shower, brushed against his shoulder.

Focus.

With a few taps, he entered the Spanish words *La Rosa de Illuminoso* into the translator app. "It says, 'the rose gives light.'"

"Where are the other clues?"

"Be right back." Jake retrieved the other artifacts from his room. After the incident with the harbormaster, he'd stopped carrying them and had hidden them carefully at the back of his dresser.

Maggie picked them up. She slid each of the original

pieces into the notches on the poker, forming a large cross. "I thought so."

Jake stuck his finger into a small hole at the top of the cross. "What do you make of this? Wait a minute … I bet the pendant goes in here. Maybe when the light passes through the ruby, we'll have another clue."

"Sounds a bit farfetched, but bring it here and let's give it a try."

Jake's cheeks flushed and he ducked, prepared for his third scolding of the day. "I can't. I sort of gave it to Julie."

Maggie leapt up, flinging her chair into the wall with the backs of her knees. "You *what?*"

"I know, I shouldn't have, but that was *before* …" The painful image of Zach and Julie kissing sprang into his mind, and he shook his head to clear it. "I'm sorry, Maggie."

Her glare pierced through him. He hoped what he said next would be enough to pacify her for the moment.

"Anyway, I bet that's how it works …" he began. "They did the same thing in the first *Indiana Jones* movie. They're Julie's favorites." He cringed as the last part slipped out.

"You Americans and your Hollywood. Not everything is like the movies, you know," Maggie said with a huff. "Why don't you just go find Julie."

Jake's shoulders sagged as he watched her stomp out of the room.

Reaching for his backpack, he hesitated, reminding himself of the harbormaster.

No. I won't bring the cross. I'll get the pendant and wait for Maggie to calm down. She deserves to be there when we connect them.

* * *

Julie opened the door of her sponsors' house. Her hair was pulled back into a ponytail, and she wore a beat-up New

York Giants sweatshirt. She quickly crumpled some tissues into her pocket.

Red eyes and her favorite sweatshirt that's never been seen in public. Uh-oh.

"What's wrong?" Jake asked.

She lunged forward and wrapped him in a forceful hug. "I'm *so* glad you're here."

Jake struggled to regain his balance, surprised by her sudden move. "Ah. Okay. Let's walk down to the park?"

"Hang on a minute." She ran inside and returned a moment later wearing a more stylish shirt and a light jacket.

They walked along the cobblestone streets in silence for nearly ten minutes until Julie finally spoke. "Zach broke up with me."

Jake attempted to connect with the countless daydreams he'd had of just this situation, and of all the clever and comforting things he'd planned to say while trying to disguise his elation. "I'm … sorry" was all he could muster.

"I've been pressuring Zach to stand up to his father. He told me he wants to spend more time writing and not as much playing football, but his dad's already talking to college scouts."

Jake bit his lip, eager to talk about the pendant but aware this was not the right moment. *Patience. She's still your best friend.* "Wasn't his dad ejected from the stands once for threatening a referee?"

"That's how intense he is." Her voice sank into a whisper. Tears dripped from her cheeks. "When I told Zach he should speak up for himself, he said if I couldn't understand his situation, we shouldn't be together."

Jake guided Julie into a small park near the ice cream store. She plopped onto a bench. "Let's rest." She patted the spot next to her, and when Jake sat beside her, she leaned her head on his shoulder. "You are a good friend, Jake. You're always there for me."

Now you notice?

"Going to high school next year is scary, isn't it?" she continued.

"Uh ... yeah, it'll be a big change."

She scooted closer to him. "We should stick together. Take the same classes and stuff. My dad knows the principal. I bet we could even get lockers next to each other."

Does she actually want this or is she just rebounding? Or trying to make Zach jealous?

She pulled her hair from its ponytail and shook her head. A strong scent of coconut shampoo drifted toward him. He waited for the familiar tingle to energize his body.

Nothing.

He inhaled again, searching for the rush of feelings he'd so often experienced.

Weird.

Julie fluttered her eyelids and smiled. Jake sat still, paralyzed. She wrapped her arms around his neck and leaned in toward him.

This is it. The moment you've been waiting for.

Emotions assaulted his mind and heart, freezing them with indecision. Julie's nose brushed against his. In a moment his first kiss would be over.

No. It's not right.

He pulled back, closing his eyes in disbelief.

"AHHHH!" Julie's shriek snapped him back to the moment.

He opened his eyes in time to see her being ripped away from him. Strong hands clamped down on his arms. Trapped, his throat tightened in fear.

Malic had Julie imprisoned in his beefy arms. She shouted,

kicked, and clawed at the brute as he carried her effortlessly toward an old Volkswagen van.

Jake wrestled and thrashed with his own attacker. His arms were useless and his feet struck nothing but air. He bit into the man's hand and warm blood washed into his mouth. The thug squealed and dropped him.

Jake stole a quick glance behind him. His apprehender was tall and skinny, with wire-rimmed glasses and a pointy nose. *It's the man Mr. O'Connell met!*

The van door slammed shut.

I've got to save Julie! Jake's mind raced to make a plan. *Two against one and I don't even have my backpack.*

He cursed—and took off at a sprint.

Hang tough, Julie. I'll find you!

Chapter 20

Jake burst through the door, flattening Maggie and scattering the contents of the suitcase she'd been carrying.

"Th-they took Julie!" he stammered.

She placed a steadying hand on his arm. "Slow down. Who took Julie?"

"*Them!*" he said, panting, barely able to breathe. He wiped the sweat and tears from his face, shook his head to clear his mind, and took a deep breath. "The men from the mountain and the church. They tried to grab me too, but I got away."

Her eyes grew wide. "You saw them?"

"Yes. The big guy, Malic ..." Jake gulped. "And the skinny one who met your dad."

The color drained from Maggie's face. "Are you sure?"

Jake related everything that had just happened, omitting the part where he and Julie had almost kissed. "We need to find her before they hurt her! Where's your dad?"

"In the back room."

He got up, barged past her, and banged against the door.

"It's no use. He doesn't answer when he's in there. And I've tried to break in already. He has the only key."

Jake retrieved his Leatherman from his backpack and opened the knife attachment. He slid the blade into the lock and twisted it, rotating the doorknob. "You forget I work at a home security shop." One final thrust and the door swung open.

Mr. O'Connell was standing at a table holding a book. He peered up, shock and confusion written across his face.

Jake dashed to one side of the table and Maggie went to the other, grabbing her father's arm. "How could you?" she cried. Tears streaming from her eyes, she began hurling his books to the floor.

Mr. O'Connell tried to stop his daughter's rampage by seizing her hands. Looking directly into her eyes, he pleaded, "What in St. Peter's are you talking about?"

"All of this skulking around on Tuesdays and Thursdays! You're a thief—a mid-week *bandit!*" Maggie sobbed.

"What? Darling, I've been taking night classes to earn my degree! I'm not spending my evenings *thieving.*" Mr. O'Connell reached for her face, but Maggie slapped away his hands.

"Classes?"

"Yes," he said, holding up a textbook. "I wanted to find a job. A *good* job, for once."

"You checked out a Spanish history book from the library," Jake said.

Mr. O'Connell nodded. "That's right. I needed to write a paper for a history class."

"But we followed you! You met one of the bandits. The skinny guy with the van ..." Maggie's voice was brimming with confusion and hope.

"Evan? Are you talking about Evan?"

"I'm talking about a skinny guy with wire-rimmed glasses, Da—I don't know his name!"

"It's Evan. He and I used to work together at my old job. You heard me talk of him, I'm sure. He also started school after being laid off. We've been carpooling."

Jake clenched his fists, desperate for anything that would help him find Julie. "He kidnapped Julie!"

Mr. O'Connell's eyes grew wide. *"Kidnapped?* Evan wouldn't kidnap anybody!"

Maggie pressed her fingers into her temples and shook her head. "Maybe you were wrong, Jake. Maybe it was someone else. It all happened so fast."

Jake shot her a sharp look. "No. It was *him.* The skinny guy with glasses and a pointy nose."

Mr. O'Connell hurried to the cabinet and pulled out a photo album. He flipped through a few pages until he found a photo of a group gathered around a picnic table. Pointing at the man in the middle, he said, "Is this the man you saw? We took this at our last company picnic."

Jake squinted, his conviction fading. "Well, it looks like him … kind of." He leaned in closer, his nose almost touching the photo. "Maybe it wasn't the same guy."

"You're sure?" Mr. O'Connell said.

Jake hoped a giant sinkhole would open up beneath his feet and take him away. "I'm sorry, sir." He shot an apologetic look to Maggie. "But we have to rescue Julie!"

"We'd better call the *Gardai,*" Mr. O'Connell said.

"Translate!" Jake cried, fury building again in his chest.

"Police." Maggie squeezed her dad. "I'm so relieved you're not a crook. But you should have told us what you were doing."

"I know, sweetheart. I'd planned to make it a big surprise. And I didn't want to get your hopes up, just in case." He kissed her cheek. "I'll go call the *Gardai.*"

"I'm really sorry," Jake said to Maggie as Mr. O'Connell left the room.

"I knew he was innocent, but all the signs pointed to something wrong." Maggie embraced Jake even tighter than her mom had before.

Must be a family trait.

He returned the hug, savoring her warmth and closeness.

Jake heard Mr. O'Connell coming back to the room and tried to pull away, but Maggie gave him a final squeeze before releasing him.

"Good news." Mr. O'Connell appeared relieved. "The *Gardai* have Julie at the station. I spoke to an officer named Fritz. He said the crooks let her go unharmed a block away. Said her sponsors were on the way, but she wanted her friends to come by as well."

The heaviness crushing Jake's chest lifted. "Thank goodness!"

"Let me call Evan and tell him I won't make it tonight, and then I'll drive you kids to see her."

"That's okay, Da. You go to your class. I can drive."

Mr. O'Connell raised an eyebrow.

"We've, um … David's car …" Maggie rolled her eyes and grinned. "It's a long story."

Chapter 21

The Cresta's bald tires screeched every time the car careened around another tight Dingle street corner. Jake's fingers had grown numb from gripping the seat. *Apparently, Maggie has inherited her father's driving skills.*

"I wonder why they let Julie go?" he asked, his feelings of relief mixing with unease. "Malic doesn't seem the type to give up. After all, he's been chasing us all over the countryside this past week."

Maggie shrugged as she steered onto a nearly deserted street. They parked the car just past the police station, and Jake took off, nearly bursting through the entrance.

The room was small, with a few chairs that acted as a waiting area and a half-wall separating that space from three desks. Behind the half-wall sat a solitary policeman, staring at a computer screen. The telltale green board of a solitaire game reflected on his glasses.

"We're here to meet our friend, Julie. She's the American who was kidnapped," Jake said breathlessly. A prickle traveled up his spine. *Something isn't right here.*

The policeman grunted as he pressed an intercom button and leaned in to speak, his eyes still focused on his game. "Fritz, those kids are here."

Several seconds later, the door behind the desk opened and a uniformed policeman emerged. "Well, good afternoon, kids. I'm Constable Fritz."

Jake's eyes traveled up to the tall man's wire-rimmed glasses. His heart slammed against his ribs. *Coincidence. It has to be.* His eyes darted to the man's hand, and he saw the thing he'd feared the most: a crisp white bandage.

Suddenly, Maggie was gripping Jake's bicep and hauling him toward the door. "We just remembered something we have to do!" she called, nearly trampling Jake in her rush for the exit. "Run!"

Fritz shouted after them and then barked orders at the other officer to catch them.

Not a chance.

Jake couldn't open the car door fast enough, and once he and Maggie were inside, he kept watch while she put the key in the ignition.

"Please start, please start," Maggie chanted as the engine turned over.

Jake looked out the back window. "Hurry!"

"*Please* st—" The roar of the engine drowned out Maggie's voice. She slammed the Cresta into gear and smoke erupted from the tires as they shot away from the curb.

Taking the quickest way out of town, they sped down a small farming road until they came to an abandoned barn, where Maggie backed the car inside and killed the engine.

Jake slammed his fist against the dashboard. "He's a policeman. The guy who has Julie is a *policeman!* He must have told his buddies to ignore anybody calling about a kidnapping." He leaned his head against the seat and closed his eyes for a moment, his mind racing through the events of the past hour. "What was that suitcase for, anyway?"

Maggie rested her forehead against the steering wheel. "I was going to give my mum a break and go help my aunt."

"You were leaving? During the treasure hunt?"

She didn't turn away fast enough to hide a tear. "You

seemed to be getting on just fine without me."

Jake felt a stab of pain slice at his heart. But also a little rush. *She's jealous. Jealous of Julie. Never made a girl jealous before.* "No way. I need you, Maggie."

"You need me?" She tilted her head slightly, her expression one of disbelief.

He nodded. "You're my friend and I can't finish this without you."

Her defenses softened and she smiled. "Thanks, Jake. I'm glad you said that."

"I hate to change the subject, but we have to save Julie! What'll we do next?"

"I say we go back to the scene of the crime and search for clues," Maggie said after a moment.

"Is that a good idea?"

"Well, we can't go to the news … Julie might be killed. And if we go to another police station, they probably won't believe us and will call back to Dingle. My parents are both away. What else can we do?"

Jake put his seatbelt back on. "Okay. Let's stop a few blocks away from the park and approach slowly."

Maggie put the car in gear and snorted, her tone giving new meaning to the term *fiery redhead.* "Actually, I'd planned to honk the horn the whole way, shouting 'come and get us!'"

Maggie flashed her eyes at Jake and he let out a laugh. He was grateful for her sarcasm, as it reduced their stress levels, if only for a minute.

*   *   *

Jake longed for camouflage as he crept alongside the thick bushes at the edge of the park. He and Maggie scanned the area for any sign that the crooks were still lurking there.

"Looks like it's clear. Come on." He led her to the bench. "This is where they grabbed you?"

Jake nodded, and he and Maggie studied the ground. A small pile of debris caught his attention. As he got closer, emotion welled up inside him. "Julie's cell phone."

He gathered up the pieces. The leather case was torn, and Jake pulled Julie's credit card from the shattered remnants. "Definitely Julie's," he said, reading the name. "She always keeps a credit card in her phone case so she doesn't have to carry a purse."

Maggie knelt and picked up a small clump of reddish dirt by her feet, crumbling it in her hands. "Did the van leave this mud?"

"I'm not sure. But that's where it was parked."

"Come on!" She was already jogging to the Cresta. "There is only *one* place on the peninsula with this red dirt—the old Corráin Castle near Dunquin!"

Jake rose and stuffed Julie's things into his backpack. "Castle?"

"Yes. It was pretty much in ruins until an American couple bought it in the late nineties. They spent their entire savings renovating it into a bed and breakfast, but then after September 11 … well, tourists stopped visiting. They went bankrupt and now the castle is sitting empty."

Maggie started the car and put it into gear.

Jake jumped into the passenger seat beside her. "Empty, except for those goons—and Julie."

Chapter 22

Jake tapped his feet the whole time, willing the Cresta to take the roads like a Formula One sports car. When they arrived, Maggie backed into a small pull-off and killed the engine. "This is a good hiding spot," she said. "Let's walk the rest of the way."

They found several big tree branches lying on the ground and used them to cover the hood of the car. Jake wiped his palms on his jeans. "Won't hide it completely, but at least it's not totally obvious."

They hiked to the edge of the forest and when they reached the clearing, Jake took in a close-up view of his first Irish castle. It was a simple but majestic stone structure with square towers in each corner. Jake's heart stopped. An old Volkswagen bus was parked near the entranceway. "There's the van!"

"I see it—she *is* here," Maggie whispered.

"But *where* exactly? This castle is huge. We can't just go barging in."

"You're right. We need a plan ..." Maggie drifted off in thought. "I've got it! The owners had to provide blueprints for approval when they proposed their renovation plans. We all got to see them at a special showing at the library."

"I like this so far," Jake said. "Go on."

"Well, I bet we can get a copy of those floor plans. But

we'll have to hurry—the county offices close in forty-five minutes," Maggie said, looking at her watch.

"Okay, then, let's go!" Jake stared at the castle for a moment as Maggie retraced her steps into the woods. *We'll be back soon to rescue you, Julie. Don't worry.*

*   *   *

For the first time since he had arrived in Ireland, being the passenger in a car driven by an O'Connell didn't make Jake ill. His singular focus was Julie. Was she scared? Was she safe? Was she still alive?

Shaking his head sternly, he banished that last thought from his mind and went back to planning her rescue. After they studied the castle's layout, they'd need to scrounge the shed for tools to break in with, maybe even go to a hardware store.

The inviting façade of a toy store suddenly caught Jake's eye and he commanded Maggie to stop. Startled by his outburst, she gasped and slammed on the brakes, and the smell of burning rubber filled their nostrils. Ignoring the honking horn and irate cussing coming from the car behind them, Jake jumped out. "I'll get some tools and take a cab back to your house. You go to the county office and find those plans!" He didn't wait for Maggie to respond.

Just as Jake reached the door of the store, an elderly gentleman behind it flipped the sign to say "Closed." Jake turned the handle but the door didn't budge.

"We're closed," the old man mouthed, pointing at the sign and then at his watch.

"But it's an emergency!"

How often can a person claim that getting into a toy store is a legitimate emergency? Jake sent a silent plea to the man.

"Sorry, lad." The clerk turned to walk away, but Jake slapped Julie's black credit card against the glass and rapped his knuckles beside it. *Anything to get inside this store.*

The man's eyes brightened. He nearly broke his wrist trying to unlock the door.

Grabbing a cart, Jake tore through the store. He ran up and down the aisles as if he were a contestant on that old *Supermarket Sweep* game show. His mind, hypersensitive to the situation, instantly formulated plans for each item he picked.

Flashlights, water balloons, whoopee cushions, silly string, slingshots, a foghorn, a battery-operated large-capacity water pistol, and a semiautomatic disc gun.

While the clerk was ringing up his purchases, a display ad caught Jake's eye:

Find Fido! Track the Signal That Emits from His Collar!

Jake yanked the radio-transmitting dog collar from the rack and tossed it on the counter with the rest of his selections.

* * *

Maggie was waiting by the door when Jake got home. "Here, quick! Take a look at the castle layout." She ushered him to the kitchen table and pointed to a room in the center of the top floor. "My guess is she's being held in here."

Jake rested his chin on his fist, analyzing the different rooms, windows, and staircases. "Why do you think that?"

"Well, when they remodeled the castle, they added windows to every room to brighten up the place. This center area is the only one with no windows."

"Good thinking." He scrutinized the map and traced a route with his finger. "I bet if we sneak in this second-story window on the south corner, we can make it in without anyone seeing."

"Agreed. We have a ladder in the barn. The two of us should be able to manage, but it would be easier if we had some help."

Jake grimaced. "I suppose desperate times call for desperate measures. I'll call Zach."

Zach completely lost his mind when he heard the news. Jake hung up and turned to Maggie. "He's in. We'll pick him up at 5:00 AM, which should be early enough for them to still be asleep but light enough for us to see what we're doing."

"What should we do 'til then?" Maggie asked.

"Do you have any chocolate syrup, flour, molasses, vegetable oil, and plastic bags?" Bewildered, Maggie put a hand on her hip. "Are we going to war or baking a cake?"

"I do make a killer cupcake," Jake chuckled.

They spent the following hours side by side, filling water balloons with syrup, pouring flour into the whoopee cushions, and loading the plastic bags with rocks.

Yawning, Jake squinted at the clock. "I've got two more things to do."

Jake filled the tank of the water pistol with a mixture of vegetable oil and molasses, creating a sticky fluid thin enough to squirt. He then pulled out his Leatherman and started taking the disc blaster apart.

"What are you doing?" Maggie asked.

"I'm going to tweak the gear mechanism to give it a little more punch. Why don't you get some rest? When I'm done, I'll try to catch a few winks myself," Jake said.

Maggie didn't argue and walked to her room.

Jake finished altering the gun. Like a Navy SEAL preparing for a mission, he organized everything in his backpack, making sure it was all easily accessible. He paused when he stumbled upon the business card the Colonel had given him.

Wonder if my great-uncle really is a colonel? Jake took a few extra seconds to commit the phone number to memory before zipping his pack.

Chapter 23

Using the hood of the Cresta as a map table, Jake walked Zach through the castle layout. He handed Zach a small copy of the floor plan that Maggie had drawn on index cards for each of them. The skin beneath Zach's eyes was puffy and dark, and his voice lacked its usual bravado. His hair, uncombed since waking, jutted in every direction, and his clothes looked as if they'd been slept in. "Okay, Jake, but what if she isn't in there?"

Jake had no alternate plan. Unable to reply, his mind stumbled over itself. Julie had to be there. He couldn't imagine what he'd do if she wasn't.

Maggie stepped in front of Zach. "She will be. Now, get in the car. Otherwise, go back to bed."

Zach stared at her for a moment, nodded, and then followed them into the car.

Maggie eased the Cresta into the same spot they'd parked in yesterday. Zach untied the ladder from the top of the car and lifted it to his shoulders as easily as if it were made of Popsicle sticks.

"You want some help with that?" Jake asked reflexively.

"You'd only slow me down." Zach moved effortlessly into the woods.

Not enjoying the competition or the gnawing sense of helplessness, Jake skirted around him and took up the lead.

He glanced back at Zach, who, even though he'd picked up his pace, wasn't even breathing hard.

Leaving the trees behind, they waded through the waist-high wild grasses that carpeted the castle grounds. When they reached the castle, Zach hoisted the ladder upright. His muscles strained as he rested it against the wall and adjusted its height to reach the second-floor window. "Ladies first."

Maggie stepped forward.

"I meant Jake."

Jake rolled his eyes. "Your girlfriend is being held captive and you're doing a stand-up routine?"

Zach shoulders sagged and he dropped the customary tough-guy persona. "I'm sorry," he groaned. "I'm not handling this well."

A few awkward seconds passed before Jake realized there weren't going to be any more quips. "Fine."

Zach braced the ladder and Jake scurried up to the window, slowing when he neared the top. His palms grew slick against the metal and his heart pounded so hard he worried the goons would hear it. He peered cautiously over the sill, searching for any sign of life. In the dim light, Jake could see that the room was empty.

At least something is somewhat easy tonight.

A quick inspection revealed the window's rudimentary design; he wouldn't have to break it. With a few quick flicks of his Leatherman, he popped the latch and eased it open. He climbed in and then poked his head back outside, waving at Maggie and Zach to join him.

Jake scanned his surroundings. The room resembled a jail cell more than a vacation spot. *Not exactly a quaint B&B.*

"Obviously, the owners never upgraded this room," Maggie said, as she slipped through the window.

"I was just thinking the same thing," Jake replied.

"Would you guys like me to find the tour guide … or can we rescue Julie and get the heck out of here?" Zach said, his voice caustic.

Seeing a light at the far end of a long hallway, Jake pressed his finger to his lips and waved to the others to follow him. Halfway down the corridor, they reached a door. Jake knelt and peeped through the keyhole.

There she is!

Julie was asleep and tied to a chair with thick ropes.

"She's in there, and she's all right," he whispered, energized by the relief pumping through him. He retrieved his Leatherman and inserted a tool into the lock. Zach grabbed it from him and pushed him aside.

"What's your problem?" Jake said, snatching it back.

Zach's lips screwed into a sneer. "You're taking forever, Grandma."

"Boys," Maggie moaned. She stepped over the tangle of struggling arms and tried the door. It swung open.

A small table lamp minus its shade sat in the corner, casting a sickly yellow glow. Jake darted to Julie and sawed at the ropes with the Leatherman's serrated blade while Zach untied the gag covering her mouth.

Julie's eyes flew open, and her face turned from fear to excitement when she realized who it was. "Wow! You …"

Maggie jammed her hand over Julie's mouth. "Shhh!"

Zach bumped Maggie out of the way, and his face softened. He knelt beside Julie and gave her a tremulous smile. "Are you okay, sweetie?"

She nodded, tears filling her eyes. "I'm so happy to see you!" She fell into Zach's arms and hugged him tightly.

Nearly oblivious to the scene that had once caused spasms of jealousy, Jake gaped at Julie's bare neck. "Where's the pendant?"

"They took it."

No. No, no, no! He clenched his teeth until his gums tingled to keep from shouting.

"Come on—let's get out of here!" Maggie led the way. But when Jake stepped over the threshold, he didn't follow the others. He turned in the opposite direction, toward the light at the end of the hall.

"Jake, no!" Maggie whisper-yelled.

"We need the pendant!"

"Your dad wouldn't want you to risk your life for this ..." Maggie tried to take hold of his sleeve, but he shrugged her off and tiptoed away.

Peeking around the edge of the slightly opened door, he saw Malic dozing in a chair. Next to him, the pendant sparkled, as alluring as a siren beckoning a sailor.

So close.

Maggie clutched him again from behind and mouthed the word "*stop.*"

Visions of his father's boat clouded Jake's mind—visions of the two of them being happy together. He turned away from her and stepped into the light.

The man's labored breathing provided the only sound. Like a deer approaching a watering hole, Jake tuned to any change in the environment. He stretched out his arm. His hand closed around the small bronze rose.

Yes!

The warmth of the sun, the smell of the Caribbean—he could almost feel the sand between his toes.

Malic gripped Jake's arm. "Mornin', lad."

Jake jammed his free hand into his coat pocket and produced the foghorn.

ARRRRRRNNNN!

The three-second burst of noise forced Malic backward,

his chair crumbling under his weight.

Jake didn't wait to see what happened next. In the seconds that followed, he bolted back down the hallway.

"Run! He's gaining on you!" Maggie cried, as she dropped out of sight below the window ledge.

Malic's heavy footsteps echoed inside the corridor. Jake dashed toward the window. The man's fingertips nipped his jacket collar, but Jake never slowed. He vaulted through the window. Catching hold of the top rung of the ladder, his momentum pulled it away from the castle wall.

Oh, no. Oh, no.

He squeezed his eyes shut as the ladder crashed to the ground like a falling tree. The thick weeds cushioned his fall, yet daggers still shot through his body. Leaving the ladder behind, Zach hauled Jake upward, dragging him toward the woods.

Pain accompanied each step as he stumbled downhill. Reaching the car, Julie and Zach piled into the backseat while Maggie frantically searched her pockets. "The keys! Where are the keys?"

"I thought you left them on the dash," Jake yelled.

"I did—I swear I did!"

Movement in front of the car caught Jake's eye.

Fritz, still in his policeman's uniform, stood dangling the keys.

"Looking for these?"

Jake locked eyes with Fritz and he spoke from the side of his mouth. "Keep your eyes on him and press the clutch ..." Below the aggressor's field of vision, he popped open the flathead screwdriver from his Leatherman. Intuiting Jake's plan, Maggie depressed the clutch and propped her other foot on the gas pedal.

Jake slid the tool into the top of the ignition. With a quick flick of his wrist, he pried the gum from the tumbler and the entire assembly spilled open.

"Now!"

He yanked the wires and touched them together, sending blue sparks into the air. As the engine caught, Maggie popped the clutch and the Cresta lurched forward.

Fritz dove out of the way as the car shot past him and sped off, tires screeching.

Chapter 24

Maggie turned onto the main road, panting, as if she were running a race. "They'll assume we've headed to Dingle. We should take the long way around the peninsula loop. The regatta begins today, so the roads will be empty and we can cruise."

"Good call." Jake retrieved the large iron cross from his backpack and placed the pendant into the hole at the end. *Perfect fit.* "Pull over."

"Why? What's wrong?" Maggie asked.

"Nothing. I want to get the pendant into the sunlight."

"But what about the crooks? We can't stop now!" Julie said.

"I'll keep watch," Zach offered. "We've been clear for miles. Let's finish this thing."

Maggie pulled the car to a stop on the side of the road. Jake set the cross on the hood and oriented it so that sunlight could shine directly on the pendant.

"Come on, come on." Jake scanned the overcast sky, refusing to believe that after everything they'd gone through, cloud cover would be the one thing standing between him and his dad's happiness.

"Maybe we should—"

"Give it a few minutes!" he snapped.

"We might not have a few minutes," Maggie said.

Jake stared at the clouds, willing them to part, but they didn't budge. He closed his eyes and hung his head.

Suddenly Zach snorted and smacked him on the back. "Check it out."

Sunlight warmed Jake's face. He fist-pumped the air, letting out a triumphant whoop. The jewel acted like a prism, cascading light onto the center part of the cross.

"It's just like in *Indiana Jones!*" Julie shouted. She pointed to the red beam of light emanating from the rose.

"What *is it* with you Americans and your movies?" Maggie said.

Jake fixed his eyes on the Spanish writing.

"*El huerfano en la mar de verde,*" Julie read.

"Translate!" they shouted.

"'An orphan in the sea of green,'" she replied.

Jake looked over at Maggie. She thrust her hands into her pockets. "Just because I live here doesn't mean I instantly know these things. When will you guys learn that?"

"Sorry." Jake pulled the cross from the hood of the car.

"But this time I do-ooh," she said in a singsong voice.

"What?" Jake ran back to her.

"Sea of green. That's probably the valley by Reask. It's the vastest pastureland on the peninsula. There are *clochans* nearby, small stone huts built thousands of years ago, like the ones the monks used on Skellig Michael," she explained.

"So they would have been here when the Spanish came," Julie said.

"Let's go!" Jake ran to open the door, paused, and then walked to the trunk of the car, following a trail of black spots.

"What is it?" Maggie asked.

"Shoot. We must have cracked the oil pan." He pointed out the fresh drips on the road. "Hope we have enough to make it home."

Maggie shot a worried look at Jake as he climbed in before starting the engine.

*   *   *

The car crested a hill, revealing an expansive open field below. Dozens of small stone walls and structures were sprinkled across it, looking from a distance like spilled salt. Jake scoured his travel book for information on the village of Reask and the *clochans.*

"One of the huts is way off by itself." Julie pointed to a beehive-shaped structure on the side of the field.

"Orphan!" Jake said, unable to contain his enthusiasm.

Maggie jerked the wheel, causing the car to veer from the road onto the high grass and toward the tiny dome-shaped building. Bouncing up and down, the Cresta groaned its displeasure.

"Who's throwing caution to the wind now?" Jake said.

Maggie jabbed his leg.

"Would you two lovebirds focus on not crashing instead of each other?" Zach said.

Jake watched Maggie's face turn a deep shade of red.

The car slid to a halt in the wet grass and Jake bolted out. He ran into the small stone structure.

Nothing. Nothing but old stone and the smell of damp grass. We've come so far for this?

Julie stood beside him. "So ... where's the treasure?"

"No idea. I didn't think it would be in plain sight. But I kind of expected a bit more than *this.*"

"Maybe this whole thing was a prank or something," Zach said.

"I can't believe anyone would go to this much trouble for a joke," Jake said.

"What do you make of this?" Julie showed them a cross that was carved into one of the stones. A tapered slit was

123

visible in the rock underneath. "I bet the cross goes in here!"

"Worth a try." Jake guided the long metal end into the opening. Nobody made a sound as they waited for something to happen.

It didn't.

Julie blushed. "Well, maybe not."

THUMP.

The sound of rock hitting rock resonated throughout the stone structure.

"The floor is moving!" Maggie shouted.

The ground beneath the cross had dropped away. After a few seconds, the movement stopped. Jake squinted and discerned a staircase leading down into the darkness. Cheers and high fives erupted inside the age-old hut.

"Must be an underground cave!" Maggie cried. "Ireland's full of them."

Jake pulled four flashlights from his backpack. Maggie directed her beam down the dark staircase and turned toward the group. "Follow me."

Chapter 25

Clustered at the bottom of the steps, the four friends shined their flashlights into the extensive cave ahead of them. Countless spider webs were illuminated, and the air was humid and stale, its dampness nearly visible. "Well, apparently, we're not done yet," Jake sighed.

"What if it's booby-trapped?" Maggie asked.

Zach stepped forward. "*Now* who's the one who's seen too many movies?"

Jake tracked some cobwebs suspended about a foot above the floor. "No, wait!" He grabbed Zach's shoulders and yanked him backwards just as a dart whizzed by Zach's face and stuck into the dirt wall on the other side of the tunnel.

Zach exhaled heavily. "As I said, maybe it's booby-trapped."

Jake stared at the remains of the tripwire.

Nobody would bother with a tripwire if there weren't something good at the end.

He wrenched the dart from the wall. "There's some sort of paint or film on the tip." He sniffed, inhaling a vaguely familiar scent. "Smells like nuts."

Maggie interjected. "Almonds, most likely. Probably some sort of primitive cyanide."

Jake was stunned.

"What? We get your crime lab shows over here, you know."

Chuckling, Jake removed his backpack and fished out a can of silly string. He shot a stream into the tunnel. The neon pink string floated to the floor and draped across many more tripwires.

"Not bad, for a twerp," Zach said.

"Step where I step and don't touch the walls." Jake lifted his foot over the first wire, ensuring his legs cleared the deadly welcome.

Two hundred feet and three cans of silly string later, they stepped out of the stifling tunnel and found themselves at the edge of a large pit. The hole was about twelve feet deep and thirty feet long.

Jake shined his light around the area. "We could try to climb down and then climb back up the other side?"

"What do you make of this?" Julie tapped her foot on a plank that extended across the pit.

"That can't be three inches wide," Jake said.

"Maybe the Spanish were skinny," Zach joked.

"Up there." Everyone followed Maggie's finger. A wider slab of wood was suspended in the air like a drawbridge from the other side. "I bet there's some way of triggering that thing to lower. They'd have to have that to get the treasure out."

Julie studied the situation. "I think I can make it across. The board isn't much different than the balance beams I use in gymnastics. Those are only four inches wide."

"I don't know, Julie. If you fell, it'd be tough to get you out of the hole," Jake said. "Not to mention, you could break your leg."

"Yeah, sweetie. I think we should come back with a ladder or something." Zach gripped her shoulder.

Julie pressed her lips together and shook her head vehemently. "I can do it. I can steady myself with those roots dangling from the ceiling. Worst case, you use rope to fish me out."

"Zach's right. We can come back." Maggie turned to walk back through the tunnel.

"I'm doing it." Julie grabbed the roots and stepped gingerly onto the plank. One foot in front of the other, she made slow but steady progress across the gap. She was nearly halfway to the other side when a loud cracking sound broke the silence.

"What was that?" Jake asked.

"I'm about to fa—" Julie lunged for a large vine as the board snapped in two.

"I'm good." She coughed as she breathed in some dirt falling from the roof of the cave.

Like a monkey on a vine, Julie shifted her weight back and forth and swung on the root she was holding. Then she let go and flew through the air, catching the next root with the opposite hand. Repeating this process, she made it the rest of the way across and dropped onto the opposite ledge.

"Hang on a minute," she called, as if nothing astonishing had just happened. A few moments later, a grinding noise sounded as the bridge lowered.

Jake led the others across the bridge.

"We'd best not tell your parents about that stunt," Jake said.

Her smile brightened the darkness. "Getting kidnapped will get me grounded for the rest of my life, anyway."

Maggie arrived and gave Julie a high five. "That was great!"

"Yeah, not bad for a girl," Zach said, as he stepped off the bridge and pulled her into his arms.

Julie grabbed Zach's collar and drew his face to hers for a kiss.

Guess they're back together. Jake waited for the familiar twinge of jealousy to wrench his gut. Nothing. He shrugged and said, "Let's go. Treasure awaits!"

Mercifully, they didn't find any more booby traps. Jake shivered as he stepped into a large chamber. "I wonder how far this tunnel goes?" Jake walked toward the tunnel that continued on the other side.

"Could be miles," Maggie replied. "Crag Cave near Killarney is nearly four kilometers long."

"Guys …" Zach said. "Over here."

Several hefty wooden chests were stacked against the wall of the cave.

"Wait, don't touch them! It might be a trap."

Zach hopped backward.

Jake picked up a small stone and threw it against one of the chests with a thud. Dust flared from the box, but nothing else happened. "Hmm. Let's open it slowly."

The boys approached the chest and each took a corner, cautiously lifting the cover.

"BANG!" Maggie shouted.

Instantly, the cover dropped, and Jake and Zach tumbled to the ground. Julie and Maggie guffawed.

"Funny. Real funny," Zach said, as he and Jake wiped the dirt from their clothes. They lifted the cover once again and a profound silence permeated the cave.

Colorful gemstones filled the box. On top lay a massive red ruby in the shape of a rose with a solid gold stem. A delicate beam of light filtered between thin fissures above, illuminating the ruby.

Jake stared at the chest, afraid to believe it was real. His throat tightened and tears formed in his eyes. "We found it," he murmured. "We *found* it!"

"Cha-ching!" Zach fell to his knees and dug his oversized hands into the jewels, his enthusiasm shaking Jake from his trance.

Zach jumped up, pumping his fist in the air. Jake turned to hug Julie and Maggie. He then felt Zach's fingers entwine with his as they slapped palms. Their eyes met, and Zach squeezed Jake's hand. "Nice going, twerp."

Jake nodded and let go. His eyes raced from one box to the next.

Twenty. There have to be twenty chests here!

"This has to be worth millions. *Millions!*" Jake's voice squeaked as the four friends moved from trunk to trunk, each one revealing bounty as rich as the next.

Julie picked up the rose from the first chest. "It's heavy! Here, Jake!"

"Wow." Jake felt the weight of the rose and rubbed his hands along the stem. He stowed the rose in his backpack. Maggie rifled through the brilliant gemstones, oohing and aahing over each find.

"Doubloons! We've got doubloons!" Zach cried, hugging Julie and Maggie. The chest he had opened was bursting with gold coins.

"No way! I wonder how much they're worth?" Jake asked, wishing he could check his smartphone for the market value of gold.

"More than you kids will ever see in your lifetime—you can be sure of that," a gruff voice boomed from behind them.

Chapter 26

Jake's heart plummeted. Malic and Fritz were standing like a police barricade between them and the exit.

"It was very kind of you to leave a trail of oil drops right to you and the treasure," Fritz said, brandishing a menacing-looking knife. "To show our gratitude, we'll kill you quickly."

"Run!" Jake yelled to the others.

"No!" Maggie said. "You can't fight them alone!"

"I'll be okay—I've got it covered!" Jake drew the squirt gun in his left hand and then whipped out the disc blaster with his right.

The crooks paused, gave Jake a quizzical look, and then laughed.

"I'm going to enjoy this," Fritz said, stepping forward.

Jake pulled the trigger on the squirt gun. The motorized pump whirled and lathered the bandits' feet in slime.

"Argh!" Fritz fell to the ground and lost his flashlight. Malic lunged toward Jake but was stopped in his tracks by a burst of high-velocity discs to the bridge of his nose. This momentary delay gave Jake enough time to cover the ground in goo, sending Malic crashing to the cave floor. When the thugs tried to regain their footing, Jake alternated between pelting them with discs and coating them with the molasses mixture. Backpedaling toward the tunnel, he concentrated his fire on Fritz's dropped flashlight. Slime and dirt bonded to the lens and sent the cavern into near darkness. Jake tossed his empty guns and flicked on his own light, smiling inwardly as he vanished into the tunnel amidst a storm of the goons' curses.

Jake ran after his friends, reaching them just a few moments later. "They'll catch up soon," he panted. "We'll have to keep moving forward. Let's hope these caves have exits as well as entrances." He pulled out a couple of whoopee cushions. Zach was baffled.

"Warning devices!" Jake whispered to him. "When they step on them, we'll hear them coming. Start blowing."

They all blew into the gag toys. Then, after preparing the passage like a minefield, they headed deeper into the cave.

Maggie took the lead, moving as fast as she dared given the dim light. Suddenly, she stopped, and the others rammed into her.

"Hey, what gives?" Zach asked.

"There's no floor!"

Jake squeezed past and shined his light toward the ground. The floor of the cave was missing, leaving only a dark black hole and a thin ledge along the side. He kicked a rock and counted. "One thousand, two th—"

SPLASH.

"One and a half seconds times thirty-two feet per second squared means it's—"

"Too far to fall," Zach interrupted.

"And this time there's no drawbridge," Julie moaned.

BRRRRPPPP! They heard the sound of the whoopee cushions popping behind them, followed quickly by incessant coughing, as the flour that Maggie and Jake had prepped the toys with assaulted the crooks' lungs.

Maggie shone her flashlight along the edge of the tunnel. "There's a small ledge. If we hug the wall, we can get past this hole." She flattened her back against the wall and slowly shuffled her feet side to side. The others followed.

As she neared the other side, Maggie's foot slipped. She fell, screaming as she plunged into the chasm.

"Maggie!" Julie cried.

She can't swim. Jake didn't hesitate. "You two keep going!" He jumped into the abyss.

The fall took much longer than the one into Blasket Sound, allowing time for images of his father to flash through Jake's mind.

Wonder if this is it.

The painful impact snapped him back to reality. He surfaced and coughed up water. Maggie was flailing next to him, desperately attempting to stay above the surface.

He wrapped his arms around her and hoisted her slightly out of the water. "Calm down—I have you. Just relax." She fought him at first but then relaxed and let him keep her afloat. His legs burned with the strain of treading water.

"Do you still have your flashlight?" he asked between breaths.

"No, I lost it."

"Okay, reach into my coat pocket. I stuffed mine in there before I jumped."

Maggie pulled the flashlight from his pocket. "Think it'll work?"

"Hope so. I paid extra for water-resistant ones."

Maggie flicked the switch and the darkness turned to light. Jake swam in a small circle, still holding Maggie while searching for an opening to the natural well. He gulped. They were completely trapped.

Suddenly, the calm surface was shattered as Zach and Julie plunged into the cistern. They popped up like buoys and shook the water from their hair.

"Whew, what a rush," Zach said.

"You idiot! You could have killed us," Jake said.

"Hey, we didn't want you two to get lonely down here."

"Ran into a dead end, didn't you?" Maggie said.

"Roger that."

"Hey, kiddies!" Malic bellowed.

Maggie snapped the flashlight off. "Shh ... don't say a word."

A rainstorm of rocks and dirt pelted them as the bandits prodded for a reaction. Nobody uttered a sound during the assault.

"Did they escape?" Malic finally asked.

"Doubt it. They're either dead or will be soon. Come on—let's grab the loot," Fritz replied.

For several minutes, the world remained black and still. The four friends treaded water, Jake still holding Maggie, trying not to make a sound.

Finally, Julie broke the silence. "I think they've gone."

Maggie flipped on the flashlight. "Yeah, but now what?"

"I feel a current. I wonder, could this be part of an underground stream?" Zach said.

Jake clawed at the water with his foot. "I don't feel a current."

"That's because your legs are twelve feet shorter than mine."

Jake didn't argue. "Okay, Zach. Take Maggie and I'll figure out where it goes."

Julie shook her head, her lips trembling. "No! It's too dangerous. What if it goes nowhere and you run out of air?"

"What choice do we have?" He handed Maggie off to Zach.

"Not a chance. You don't get all the glory here. I'll go."

"It's not about glory!" Jake said.

Zach's eyes darkened with sincerity, and every trace of machismo left his voice. "Listen. I *should* go. If I don't make it, it'll take your brain to figure a way out of this mess."

Julie stifled a sob. Jake nodded slightly, amazed by this first show of respect after years of feuding. "Take the rope from my backpack. It's about forty feet long. We'll hold the other end and use it to guide you back."

Zach swam over to Jake and dug into his backpack. He fished out the rope and handed one end to Julie, looping the other around his waist. He sucked in a deep breath and then dove under the water.

Silence filled the well once again.

Jake treaded water, really struggling now with the weight of Maggie and the heavy rose in his backpack. He wanted to ignore the pain and the fatigue to focus on what to do next, but it was impossible.

The calm surface of the water broke and Zach's head appeared. "Game on."

"You found something?" Julie said, breathless with relief.

"There's a cavern with air and dry ground on the other side of this wall. I tied the rope to one of those thingies that grows from the ground."

"Stalagmites," Maggie interjected.

"Right. Thanks for the geology lesson, Professor. Can we skip chapter two and just use the rope to guide us out of here?"

Everyone laughed.

Genuine pride shone in Zach's eyes. *No false bravado. Good for him.* "Nice going. Will you take Maggie first? My legs are spent."

"You got it, bro."

Maggie draped her arms around Zach's neck. He held the rope. "Ready?"

She nodded, and they both took deep breaths before plunging under the water. Julie left next, followed by Jake.

Swimming in darkness wasn't new to him, but knowing he was trapped under tons of rock added a whole new dimension to his fear.

For Zach to have kept swimming—not knowing if there was an opening at the end—took serious courage.

The rope led him through a tunnel and then sloped upward; Jake kicked to accelerate, his lungs begging for release. His head cleared the surface of the water, and he gasped for air. Relief washed over him as he spotted Maggie, sitting on the shore and holding a flashlight. He crawled out of the murky pool and collapsed onto dry ground next to the others.

"This is incredible. We're probably the first people ever to see this place—the first ever in the entire world ..." Julie marveled.

"Not too many places are left untouched," Jake agreed.

Maggie shined her flashlight beyond them. Yet another tunnel. "We'll find a way out of this cave, or I'm not an O'Connell."

Jake struggled to his feet and offered his hand to Maggie. "We're soaked and the temperature can't be more than fifty degrees in here. Hypothermia will set in soon. Let's go, Miss O'Connell."

They walked for another hour until the floor began to decline sharply. "This doesn't seem right," Maggie said. "We're walking deeper underground."

"Switch off your light! I see something," Zach called from the rear as he hurried past the girls to the front. "I thought so. There's light down there."

He walked swiftly ahead and the others hustled to keep up with him. Soon the tunnel became steeper and more slippery.

"This clay is slick ... Hold up, Zach!" Julie said.

Her cautionary words came too late. Maggie slipped and

tumbled, mowing down the others like bowling pins. The mass of arms and legs picked up speed. Sliding on his back, Jake struggled to right himself and spun just in time to see the tunnel open up into bright daylight.

His mind raced to process what he was seeing as he fell through the air: crashing ocean, hundreds of feet below.

Not good.

Chapter 27

"Gotcha!" Zach caught Jake's collar, and he dangled like a pendulum, his body slamming against the cliff.

Don't … look … down.

Of course, the moment the thought hit him, Jake did look down. His stomach lurched, and he shut his eyes.

Maybe up would be a better place to look.

Zach was holding onto him with one arm and onto a tree root with the other. Maggie was clutching a small tree, and Julie was clinging to Maggie's legs. *How long can they hang there like that?*

A goat stood on a rocky ledge a few feet to the left of the cave's mouth, grazing on the wild grasses. Without any sense of urgency, it swiveled and bounded up the mountain.

"Zach, can you swing me over to the ledge where the goat was?" Jake shouted. "There's a trail to the top." He didn't know what he'd do if the answer was no.

Seconds later, he was swaying side-to-side, gaining momentum with each upswing.

Probably a good thing my stomach is empty.

With a final jarring yank, Jake soared skyward and slammed to the ground. Closing his eyes, he clasped his hands together. "Thank you, thank you, thank you," he whispered.

Now get to work.

Kneeling with his legs wide, he yanked the rope from his bag and tied one end to a thick root protruding from the face of the cliff. He tossed the other end to Zach, who looped it through the stronger root he clung to, and hurled the remaining slack to Maggie and Julie. Julie climbed up Maggie's back and grabbed it.

"You'll have to swing," Jake called to Julie. He jammed his arm into a crack in the rock for support and prepared to catch her. "Shouldn't be a big deal after the stunt you pulled in the cave."

"Yeah, but that was only twelve feet off the ground!" she said … and then soared through the air.

Jake caught her with his free arm, relief sweeping over him. "Can you make it up the hill on your own?"

She nodded, wide-eyed, her entire body quivering. She let go of the rope and climbed up the steep incline.

Zach pulled the rope toward him and threw it to Maggie. "Your turn."

She took the rope, swung to Jake, and headed up the hill behind Julie.

Jake didn't have time to prepare for Zach. A Tarzan yell shattered the silence, and Jake turned to see Zach coming at him full tilt, his mouth wide and his legs bent. He toppled Jake with a thud, but somehow he kept his balance enough to give Jake a noogie before following Maggie up the hill.

Cresting the cliff's edge, Jake found the others sprawled on the grass, panting and speechless under the dazzling Irish sun. He collapsed next to Maggie and stared up at the azure sky.

"Have you ever seen anything as lovely as this?" Maggie said. Her red curls were splayed in the grass, her green irises sparkled like gemstones, and her cheeks glowed pink, even under a layer of soot and dirt.

Electricity zinged up Jake's spine. *Yes. I think I have.*

* * *

"Zach, I have to make a confession," Jake said, as they trudged across a thick grassy pasture. The girls lagged behind, searching for a four-leaf clover.

Zach frowned. "What?"

This is it. Let the pummeling begin. Jake wiped his sweaty hands on his jeans and his eyes met Zach's. "I stole your novel from your duffle bag."

Zach blinked but squeezed his fists at his sides and kept walking. "I wondered where it went. Remind me to kill you if we live."

Jake didn't hear any real threat or concern in Zach's voice. "The thing is, I thought it was great. And I was kind of hoping to read the rest ..."

Zach stopped, his forehead knitted together. "You liked it?"

"Yeah. It was awesome. I want to find out what happens."

"Good luck with that. I'm done writing," Zach said, a regretful edge to his voice. He resumed walking.

Jake jogged to catch up with him. "Why? You've got talent. You shouldn't give up."

"It's not that simple." This time Zach's voice and posture grew so stiff that Jake decided not to push him any further.

They rounded a bend and a large flock of sheep blocked their path. Zach stopped abruptly, grimacing. "What the ...?"

The boys stood for a few minutes, covering their noses and waiting for the girls to catch up before braving the turbulent sea of wool. There was a road ahead, and an old barn was visible on the opposite side. Jake hoped they had a phone.

"Hey, we found one," Julie smiled triumphantly and extended her hand, revealing a four-leaf clover.

The sound of an engine sputtered over the hill, mingling with the bleating of the sheep.

"Your luck is working already! I hear a car," Jake said.

They all turned toward the road—waving, whistling, and cheering.

As the beat-up van crested the hill, Jake dropped his arms. *Malic and Fritz.*

Zach cursed as the engine gunned and the vehicle raced toward them. "Whatever happened to the luck of the Irish?"

"Guys, run to the barn!" Maggie said, moving quickly and hitting the sheep on their hindquarters. The flock scattered onto the gravel road. "I'll slow them down."

Jake hesitated, but Maggie's expression implored him to go. He ran down the hill after Julie and Zach.

In the barn was an old wagon the size of a compact car. Its wooden wheels were wrapped with thin iron strips. Jake figured it had last been used during the potato famine.

But wheels are wheels.

"Get in the wagon!" he yelled to Julie. "Zach, you push ... we can ride it down the hill and put some distance between us and the crooks!"

Jake joined Julie in the wagon, holding up the hitch and doing his best to steer. Zach braced his shoulders against the rear and grumbled, advancing the ancient cart forward. The wheels creaked as they rolled, gathering momentum with each step Zach took. Maggie arrived, took one look at the situation, and helped Zach push it toward the sloping road, where it began to pick up speed downhill. Then they hurdled over the sides and jumped in, panting.

Behind them, the van had cleared the mutton roadblock and was beginning to accelerate. The wind whipped Jake's hair and stung his skin. He squinted to shield his eyes.

"They're getting closer!" Maggie yelled. "What's the plan?"

"Take control!" Jake called to her.

Maggie scrambled to the front and grabbed the hitch. Jake tore open his backpack.

"I've got slingshots!" he said to Zach. "You any good with them?"

"Who do you think knocked out the scoreboard after we lost to East Middle School?"

"I thought so. Here's the ammo." Jake opened the sandwich bags full of rocks and syrup-packed water balloons. "Wait until they get really close."

Zach nodded and the boys crouched on their knees, watching the van close the distance between them. Fritz's lecherous grin was now visible just fifty yards away.

"Now?"

Jake shook his head.

Twenty-five yards.

"Now?" Zach called again.

Jake stared at the van.

Five yards.

Jake rose onto his knees, his slingshot armed. "Now!"

Jake's balloon struck the passenger side of the windshield, coating it with chocolate syrup. Zach's rocks struck the glass on the driver's side. It shattered, and Malic swerved and slammed on the brakes.

"Nice shot!" Julie cried.

Zach and Jake high-fived each other.

But Malic and Fritz managed to kick the windshield out onto the hood. The van veered back onto the road and accelerated once again.

"Can't this wagon go any faster?" Zach yelled.

"Uh, guys?" Julie grabbed Zach's shirt and pointed straight ahead. The road switched back to the right in a tight U-turn. The embankment slanted slightly, forming a racetrack-like curve.

Jake cringed, pretty certain they lacked the proper safety equipment to survive a wagon crash. "Move to the right side of the wagon!" he shouted to the others. Climbing over the railing, he stood on the narrow ledge where the wagon's box was bolted to the frame. He gripped the wood and leaned back. The wagon started to tilt and the left wheels lifted slightly off the ground.

"More! We need to lean more!"

The other three slid over as far as they could. As they rapidly approached the switchback, Jake groaned, shifting his weight even farther to raise the wheels.

Thank goodness for sailing lessons.

The van came up behind them, engine revving, and Malic's lips curled into a shark-like leer.

Like a sailboat in a stiff wind, the wagon tipped to nearly forty-five degrees, its left wheels connecting perfectly with the embankment of the switchback. It blasted around the turn like a bobsled.

Malic's eyes widened wildly as he realized he'd misjudged the curve. With tires screeching, and leaving a trail of blackened rubber on the pavement, the van careened into the side of the hill. Steam billowed above its crumpled hood.

The four friends cheered as the wagon righted itself at the end of the turn and continued down the hill. As they rolled out of sight of the van, Jake saw Malic and Fritz trying to pry the bent fenders away from the van's tires.

"Something tells me they'll be back."

Chapter 28

Maggie pointed ahead of them. "Guys, we have another problem."

The wagon had picked up considerable speed and was racing toward another switchback. Only a flimsy guardrail separated the road from the cliff.

Jake groaned, wondering what he'd done to deserve this. "We need to jump before it goes over!"

Maggie shook her head, eyes wide with panic. "We're going too fast to jump! We have to slow down!"

"Can't you use the brake?" Julie asked.

"There *is* no brake!" Maggie cried.

"That's what *you* say." Zach grabbed the wagon rail and climbed out, jamming his left foot against the steel-rimmed wheel.

Jake helped Zach steady himself as he applied more pressure. There was a stench of burning shoe rubber and the wagon began to slow down.

"It's working!" Jake yelled.

He quickly assessed the upcoming cliff. "It's now or never, guys. Bend your knees, tuck your chin, and cover your head with your arms!"

Maggie and Julie leapt from the rail and rolled end-over-end into the ditch. Maggie winced as she held up a thumb, and then she collapsed.

"Come on, Zach!" Jake shot from the wagon and

somersaulted to a stop. But when Zach jumped, his foot slipped and was sucked between the wheel and the frame. The sound of breaking bones resonated like gunshots.

Oh, no.

Jake watched in horror as the wagon bounced down the hill, dragging Zach's limp body toward the edge of the precipice. At the very last moment, it released its passenger, hit the guardrail, and disappeared over the cliff.

Jake ran to Zach. Bloody scrapes covered his body and his ankle was bent into a nasty L-shape. He moaned and curled inward. "My dad's going to kill me."

He nearly died and he's worried about his father's reaction?

The girls arrived, and Julie wrapped her arms around Zach. Jake spotted a barn just a few hundred feet away. It had a small fenced corral on one side. "Let's head across the field to that barn. Maybe we can hide in there." The three of them helped Zach to his feet.

Zach's body protested with each step, shaking from the unimaginable pain, but he never so much as whimpered.

Tough guy.

They entered the barn through a small door and Jake locked it behind them. A familiar scent washed over him.

"Horses! We can ride them the rest of the way into town," Maggie said with relief. She slung a saddle over her shoulder, opened one of the stalls, and with the expertise of a rodeo queen, saddled a massive white mare. Then, releasing the horse from its stall, she grabbed another saddle from the railing.

Jake stood frozen, his focus locked on the horse. "What are you doing?"

"Don't just stand there," Maggie said. "Help me!"

"Maggie ... th-there has to be another way."

"This is the *only* way, Jake! Zach can't walk. I doubt we'll find a house for miles—and those thugs will be here any second!"

"I can't do it. My–my dad, he ... you *know* about me and horses!"

Maggie dropped the saddle and looked Jake squarely in the eye. "This is different."

"Listen to me, Maggie! He was showing me how to jump and his horse screwed up. I don't trust them—I can't do it!"

Maggie marched over and put her hands on Jake's shoulders. "Jake. Please. Those goons will be here soon!"

The large door creaked open and Maggie's face blanched.

"Sooner than you think." Fritz stepped inside, grinning.

Julie screamed and ran toward a door on the other side of the barn. Jake and Maggie grabbed Zach, who was already hopping after Julie. They reached the door and struggled against it, but it wouldn't budge.

"We're trapped!" Maggie said.

Malic and Fritz were creeping toward them, wary of any more tricks.

Julie gave Jake a little push. "Jake, you have to ride for help."

"Yeah, Jake. Go!" Zach said.

"I'm not leaving you guys behind!"

"*Is fear rith maith ná drochsheasamh,*" Maggie exclaimed.

"Translate?"

"*Celtic Run.* A clan saying. It means 'a good run is better than a bad stand.'" Maggie grabbed Jake's arm. "Go, Jake."

Resigned, Jake nodded. He turned toward Maggie. "Before I go ..."

He placed his shaking hands on either side of her face and pulled her to him. His eyes closed. Their lips met and fire blasted through his veins—the reality of their situation momentarily eclipsed by the thrill of his first kiss.

Slipping the radio dog collar into Maggie's jacket pocket,

Jake gazed into her eyes. "I won't let you down." He let go and sprinted directly toward the bandits.

Fritz and Malic spread their arms and legs. Jake's eyes locked with Fritz's and he ran straight at him, ready to become a human snowplow. Just before impact, he veered to the left and dove between Malic's legs. With a quick forward roll, he was back on his feet and racing for the barn opening. Fritz spun and chased after him.

The white horse had wandered out to the corral and was chewing some foliage next to a stack of barrels.

"Hi-yah!"

The horse's ears perked. Jake jumped onto a barrel and sailed into the saddle. He dug his heels into the horse's sides. "Giddy-up!"

As Fritz's gloved hand swiped for Jake, the horse leapt into action, accelerating with astounding speed.

Remarkable horse.

Surprisingly at ease, Jake aimed the mare toward the corral fence. The moments before his father's accident replayed in his mind.

"Lean forward, son. Heels down, so they don't slip out of the stirrups. Knees into the saddle and look forward. Watch me do it first …"

Jake's jaw locked tight as fifteen hundred pounds of sheer muscle beneath him contracted to propel them both over the fence. Then the horse's hooves slammed into the ground on the other side.

Thanks, Dad.

He glanced back at the barn and saw Fritz running for the crunched-up van.

Hang in there, gang.

Jake leaned forward in the saddle, digging in his heels, as the horse bounded across the open fields toward Dingle.

Chapter 29

The sound of horse hooves clattering against cobblestone echoed throughout the deserted streets.

Where is everyone?

A twinge of fear clutched at Jake's chest.

Oh, right—the Dingle Regatta. Maggie said most of the town would be there today. He looked around and spotted a pay phone by the door of a closed pub.

Good thing they still have a few of those around.

He picked up the receiver, deposited some coins, and dialed the Colonel's number.

* * *

The sound of the ocean crashing on the other side of the massive building was deafening. His nerves steeled, Jake walked through the empty parking lot until he reached the fish-processing plant. A sign on the door read "Closed."

Jake had tracked Maggie and the others for miles to the seaside factory, locating it easily with the radio dog collar.

An excellent product. I should give it five stars.

Taking a deep breath, he crept to a section of wall that had rotted with time. Little by little, he pried a loose board away and crawled in. Tiptoeing behind some boxes, he spotted his friends lying on the gray stone floor.

They're still alive!

Nearby, a conveyor belt fed a frighteningly large and filthy machine. Spider webs hung from a metal catwalk twenty feet overhead. Jake watched Maggie swivel her head all around, as if searching for someone.

"I'm sorry, dearie. The cannery'll be closed all weekend," Fritz chuckled. "Ain't no one here but us and some rotting fish."

"What are you going to do with us, you manky git?"

Suddenly, another man appeared. "Miss O'Connell, 'tis not proper language for a fine Irish lass."

"Shamus!" Maggie gasped, glaring at the museum curator. "*You're* involved in this?"

"Aye. And now, here we are—all together—minus one, that is." Shamus darted a scornful glare at Fritz and Malic.

"Jake got away, so your plans are over," Julie said.

"Only delayed, sweetheart. Only delayed. I have to hand it to you. I'd lost the trail until the harbormaster called me about an artifact some kids had taken off Skellig Michael. Good thing he read me the second clue," Shamus said, his eyes hardening to an onyx cast.

"So, that's how your goons followed us to Mount Brandon," Maggie said.

Shamus smiled. "Aye, but they botched that, as well." He shot another contemptuous eye at his minions. "But Dingle is a small town, so I figured if we watched the park by the ice cream shop long enough, one of you would show up sooner or later."

Maggie struggled against the ropes binding her arms tightly to her side. "Jake'll stop you, you know."

Hearing that, Jake felt a rush of pride.

"Well, my dear, we'll just see about that." Shamus walked over to the conveyer belt and threw the control switch, activating the huge metal blades at the end of the machine.

"After one of you watches your other friends ground into can-sized chunks, you'll tell us where to find the last little troublemaker." Then turning toward his coconspirators, he murmured, "And once we've finished them off, we'll be able to take the treasure and sail far, far away from this wretched island."

Fritz and Malic moved toward them, exuding evil.

Julie screamed. Zach struggled to free his hands. Maggie tried to crawl away, but Malic grabbed her and easily carried her over to the humming conveyor belt. She spat and fought, but his grip was too strong.

Rage boiled up inside Jake.

"STOP!" His voice boomed, reverberating inside the cavernous factory.

Malic and Fritz stopped.

"Who's there?" Shamus hissed.

"Over here." Jake calmly strode toward the group. He adjusted his newly acquired Dingle Rugby Team hat.

Shamus's eyes simmered. "Not sure how you got here, but thanks for saving us so much trouble. In fact, you've been nothing but helpful these past few days," he grinned. "Now, Malic." Shamus's tone turned icy cold.

Jake pointed at Maggie. "Let her go and I'll let you live. If even a hair of hers touches that conveyor belt, it'll be you leaving the factory in cans."

Malic and Fritz looked at each other and then burst out laughing. Shamus clapped Fritz's shoulder and drummed on the police radio sitting on the crate. "Hear anything?"

"No, boss. I've had it on scan all day. If he went to the *Gardai*, we'd have heard about it."

Shamus grinned. He nodded to Fritz, who walked toward Jake. "This isn't one of your American Westerns, laddie. No cavalry is riding in to save you here."

Jake smiled and winked at a very confused Maggie. "The cavalry? How about the Defense Force, Army Ranger Wing?"

He stuffed two fingers into his mouth and whistled.

With precision, a dozen commandos rappelled through the skylights and glided through the nearby windows. Fritz reached for his knife but froze when he saw scores of laser dots floating on his chest. He raised his hands in surrender.

Shamus bolted for the door. But Julie's foot flew out in front of him, dropping him to the ground with a painful yelp.

"Way to go, sweetie!" Zach said.

Malic lifted Maggie in front of him, and using her as a human shield, ran for the door. Two Rangers sprinted after him with Jake close behind. But before they could reach him, Malic ran through it. The sound of the bolt slamming home boomed throughout the factory. A Ranger banged his booted foot against the door, but it didn't budge.

"Hoist me up!" Jake pointed to the catwalk that led to the other room. The Rangers interlocked their fingers and knelt. Jake jumped, his feet landing on their hands, and their powerful arms heaved him skyward. He caught the lower rail of the catwalk and pulled himself up.

Swiftly and stealthily, he snuck into the other room and scanned the area for movement. The room was as vast as the one he'd just left and full of equipment. Malic was heading for a forklift, with Maggie still in his clutches, kicking and screaming. Jake sprinted down the catwalk. The long room opened up to the ocean and Jake could see a boat docked alongside the pier. *Can't let Malic get there.*

The forklift's engine belched and roared to life.

I'm not going to make it in time.

Ahead, a pulley system dangled at the edge of the walkway, gently swaying in the breeze.

"Jake!"

Maggie's shriek fueled him. He ran faster and harder than he'd ever run before. At the end of the catwalk, he leaned out to grab the pulley.

Too far.

Thinking fast, Jake reached for his yo-yo and cast it toward the pulley. It sailed true and wrapped around the hook. A quick yank and the pulley was in Jake's hands.

Let's hear it for fishing line instead of string. Here we go.

The contraption hummed so loudly it hurt Jake's ears, and the friction of the wire against the wheels caused sparks as he rode the pulley down. Glimpsing the forklift between his feet, he landed hard on its back end. He fell to his knees but maintained his balance on the moving machine.

Malic spun around in the driver's seat and drew his knife. He slashed at Jake, and a sharp pain shot through his wrist. Jake dodged another swipe, dove on top of Malic, and deftly fastened the pulley's hook to the thug's belt. Before Malic could react, Jake grabbed Maggie and rolled off the machine.

The wire snapped tight, ripping Malic from the forklift. Jake and Maggie watched as the unmanned machine rolled out of the building and careened off the pier, directly into the ocean. They glanced back to see Malic dangling in the air, with two rangers quickly approaching him.

"Maggie," Jake whispered, still shaking from the shock and the adrenalin. "Are you okay?"

They had both sustained numerous cuts and bruises from their fall, but her green eyes brightened.

"*Is tú mo ghrá,*" she said.

"Translate?"

"It means this."

She kissed him.

Chapter 30

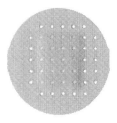

The paramedic dabbed antiseptic on the cuts on Jake's arm. He winced as the ointment began to do its work, stinging his sensitive nerve endings.

The previously deserted factory parking lot had transformed into a hornet's nest of Army Rangers, police officers, and reporters, every one of them working to piece together the sequence of events that ended in the commando raid.

Jake took off his hat and smiled at the tiny camera inserted against the visor. It had been his idea to wear a device that provided a video feed to the Rangers, ensuring they could see the exact location of the crooks and have documentation of everything that happened.

Zach's pale body was strapped to a gurney, his gnarled ankle splinted and ready for the journey to the hospital. A paramedic carrying an IV drip bag wheeled him to the waiting ambulance.

Maggie and Julie stood about twenty feet away, getting checked by paramedics while being questioned by the *Gardai*. Maggie's gaze darted to Jake every few seconds.

An engine backfired, and seconds later the O'Connells appeared. They parked and rushed to Maggie, their arms outstretched and tears staining their cheeks. Once Maggie had been appropriately squeezed and scolded, Mrs. O'Connell turned her attention to Jake.

"Oh, my dear, what you must have been through! How horrible!"

A taxi van honked as it wove its way through the crowd, pulling to a stop near the four children.

"Mom! Dad!" Julie jumped and ran to the van, not heeding the entreaties of the medic to remain still.

"Sweetheart!" Julie's dad pulled her into his arms. He jerked his thumb behind him at Zach's parents, who were also climbing out of the vehicle. "We took the company jet together after Mr. O'Connell called us last night."

Zach's father waited patiently for his wife to finish doting on their son. Then he lightly squeezed Zach's shoulder. "You okay, son?"

Zach swallowed hard. "I broke my ankle, Dad. Not sure it will be healed in time for the first game."

His father and mother exchanged a quick but meaningful look. "It's okay, son," his dad said earnestly. "Football isn't everything. Maybe this will give you some time to work on your book."

Zach grabbed the gurney railing and hoisted himself to a sitting position, wincing with every movement. He held out his arms to hug his father, his eyes shining with unshed tears.

Jake smiled as he watched the unexpected scene, and Maggie's hand touched his shoulder. "We'll call your da when we get home to let him know you're all right."

"No need," Julie's mom said. "He came with us on the jet."

A handicap-accessible van pulled up behind the first taxi. The sliding door opened, and Jake's dad rolled toward him, his arms open.

"Dad!" Jake ran to his father and hugged him tightly.

"Why, the last time I saw you, you weren't any bigger than Jakey here." A booming voice broke through the crowd. The

Colonel bent down to wrap his strong arms around Jake's father. "Your boy here is quite the hero."

"I know. I've always been proud of him," Jake's father said, looking up at his son, his voice cracking with emotion.

Jake pulled out his smartphone and snapped a picture.

"What are you doing?" his dad asked.

"I want to show that bartender that the Colonel really does run an army unit."

"Ach, never mind that, lad. I shouldn't have been boasting about my work to that ale slinger anyway." The Colonel patted Jake on the back. "Besides, I'm hitting retirement age next month. They'll soon be forcing me out."

One of the rangers called to the Colonel and he excused himself for a little while. Jake turned to his father and looked at him. He was going to tell him all about the treasure and how they could buy back their sailboat now, but feeling his father's strong embrace suddenly made it all seem trivial.

I didn't realize how much I missed him.

My dad, and not a boat ... that's what I need.

Epilogue

Jake bit his bottom lip as the wheels of the aircraft left the ground. It had been an emotional goodbye, harder than he had imagined. Once a kid who had always looked to the future, Jake was surprised by how much he didn't want his time in Ireland to end.

The press coverage over the past six weeks had been intense. Fueled by the desire for positive publicity, the Irish government had streamlined their legal processes and awarded the kids their share of the treasure within a week.

Jake looked over at Julie as she rested her head on Zach's shoulder. He smiled, glad for them. Zach and Julie, whose families were already well-off, had chosen to donate their shares to several charities and institutions in Ireland, including the Dingle Museum, which would now house the Santa Maria de la Rosa exhibit, helmed by a new museum curator. Zach and Julie had stipulated one condition as part of their donation: the museum must hire Mr. McGreevy as architect for the modifications that would be required to display the extensive new exhibit.

During one of the many press interviews, Jake had dropped a comment about Zach's writing ability. Agents were soon competing to sign Zach, who was already working on a novel detailing their summer adventure. He intended to keep playing football after his ankle healed, but the game no longer limited his life.

Jake watched as Zach leaned over to remove something from his duffle. He instinctively held it at arm's length, wary of any booby traps. Jake winked at him. While their mutual ribbing and pranks continued, it was now under the flag of friendship, not conflict.

Julie smiled at Jake. She pulled out a magazine highlighting the upcoming summer Olympics and started leafing through it. After reflecting on her acrobatic accomplishment in the tunnel, Julie had decided she loved gymnastics more than any other sport. Jake was confident that, although she was getting a late start, she would be gracing gymnastic magazine covers in just a few short years.

Mr. McGreevy had intended to return to New York after the hubbub over the rescue had died down, but Mrs. O'Connell wouldn't hear of it. Jake had moved out to the sofa, giving his dad David's bedroom. Whether it was the feeling of being useful again or Mrs. O'Connell's excellent cooking and care, Mr. McGreevy had made more progress in his physical therapy in the few weeks in Ireland than in the entire previous year in New York.

The Colonel was often at the house with more distant relatives to introduce. As foretold, the army had forced him to retire, but Jake's dad had asked him to come to New York for a while to help out. Jake was thrilled, as the Colonel had already begun teaching him hand-to-hand combat and other Ranger techniques. If this summer had taught Jake anything, it was that he needed to be prepared for any situation.

Already feeling nostalgic, Jake turned his smartphone to airplane mode and flipped through the photos he'd taken. The first one he pulled up showed Shamus doing the perpwalk as the police carted him out of the fish factory. Fearful of how he'd be treated as a policeman in prison, Fritz had struck a deal. In exchange for solitary confinement, he'd ratted on

Shamus, ensuring a guilty verdict, and provided the location of all of the stolen artifacts.

Jake swiped his finger across the screen and landed on Patrick, the tinker, dressed in sixteenth-century Spanish garb and standing alongside a giant mural depicting their summer adventure. Jake had arranged for the Dingle Museum to hire Patrick as Shamus's replacement. Patrick had quickly grown to fill the role. His accomplished storytelling and easygoing nature were a big hit with the visitors. Patrick and Darcie's daughter was now enrolled in school and the family had rented a house in Dingle, their first real home.

Jake could almost smell the hay when he scrolled to the next photo. It was of the white mare he had ridden to escape the crooks. When he returned the horse, it had taken some sweet-talking and a few gold doubloons to calm the angry owner down. Afterwards, Jake had spent several more afternoons at the farm, rediscovering the joys of horseback riding with Maggie.

The next photo was of a construction crane lowering a sign that read "Maggie's" above the pub. Maggie had set aside enough money to pay for her college, and then spent the rest purchasing a local auto repair shop for her brother and the pub for her parents. Her parents had been adamant about her keeping the money, but she'd won the argument. The O'Connells, true to form, then revised the deed of ownership, placing it in Maggie's name.

Mr. O'Connell finished his degree and took over managing the pub's books during the day and helped tend bar at night. Mrs. O'Connell redecorated the entire place and changed up the menu, adding a traditional American hamburger called "The McGreevy" in honor of Jake. To commemorate their adventure, she also added some Spanish fare, as well as a dessert called "The Rose": Cake, in the shape of a rose, topped with a cherry mousse. It soon became Dingle's favorite after-dinner treat.

Jake scrolled through the pictures until he came to one of Maggie wearing her Irish Dance Academy T-shirt. Unbeknownst to her, Jake had submitted the video of her outstanding dance that night to one of the most prestigious dance schools in the United Kingdom.

The day the thick envelope arrived in the mail would go down as one of Jake's favorite memories. Maggie's smile and tears of joy were rivaled only by the pride glowing in her parents' faces. Jake had contemplated sending the application to Julliard so that she could study in New York, but he knew that that would have been selfish. Maggie belonged to Ireland.

Jake chuckled when he got to the picture of him and the harbormaster. It turned out that the man wasn't involved in the crooked gang after all, and had only called Shamus because he was a museum curator and might have known what to do with the artifact. Once Jake had learned this, he immediately felt bad for ruining the innocent man's living area, so he purchased an up-to-date kitchenette for him, complete with a new set of china and glasses, a state-of-the-art dishwasher, and a much sturdier baker's rack.

With college funds safely stashed in an interest-bearing account, Jake carved out the amount to buy back their old family sailboat and called several boat dealers in an attempt to track it down. With luck, they would have it by next spring.

Jake spent most of his final weeks in Ireland helping the O'Connells remodel the pub. In the evenings, he was busy going over designs for the museum with his dad. And while they went over the plans, they talked … about Ireland and their newly discovered relatives, about sailing and horseback riding, and about baseball and life. They even spoke about

Jake's mother. She had died when Jake was very young, and the loss was still evident in Mr. McGreevy's voice.

Jake knew it paled in comparison, but he too was feeling the sting of love lost. The night before he left, he and Maggie spent hours discussing their past and their future. Theirs had by no means been a typical romance, forged as it was under stress and in danger. It was unique, much like the Island of Emeralds itself.

Now the two would be an ocean apart. But their friendship would endure. They would write to each other, they would call each other, and one day, they would see each other again—perhaps on another adventure.

*   *   *

It was Zach who first noticed that Jake was significantly taller. Jake realized he had grown, and although the true measurement was only two inches, he found himself almost eye-to-eye with Zach. His commanding new stature didn't stem so much from the physical growth as from the improvement in confidence and poise. The many acts of courage he displayed had made him a young man. He was wiser too, more able to enjoy the subtle pleasures in life.

There had been no Caribbean sunsets that summer, no tropical breezes, and no hoisting of sails with the wind in his face. And yet, Jake knew it had been the best summer of his life.

Made in the USA
Charleston, SC
06 August 2012